November 2001

For the Redwood Library,

from Naomi Glink Zucker

BENNO'S BEAR

Benno's Bear

N. F. ZUCKER

Dutton Children's Books ✌ New York

Library of Congress Cataloging-in-Publication Data

Zucker, Naomi Flink.
  Benno's bear / by N. F. Zucker.—1st ed.
    p. cm.
  Summary: After being arrested as a pickpocket, Benno is separated from his father, who is sent to prison, and from the bear he had helped to raise and had come to love, when he is taken in by a kindly policeman and his wife.
  ISBN 0-525-46521-9
  [1. Pickpockets—Fiction. 2. Bears—Fiction. 3. Fathers and sons—Fiction.] I. Title.
PZ7.Z7795 Be 2001
[Fic]—dc21 2001028537

Published in the United States by Dutton Children's Books,
a division of Penguin Putnam Books for Young Readers
345 Hudson Street, New York, New York 10014
www.penguinputnam.com

Designed by Alyssa Morris
Printed in USA • First Edition
10 9 8 7 6 5 4 3 2 1

For Naftali

He giveth goodly words

Contents

BENNO'S BEAR

1

The Bear and the Fly

THE BEAR WAS MOANING, low like the winter wind. I could hear her through the stone wall of the cell. A fly crawled along the wall. It shouldn't have been there, in a stone cell, in the middle of winter. The fly was like me—small and ugly, with skinny legs that twitched and jumped, and eyes everywhere.

My legs were no good to me now. They were fast, but where could they carry me? Two steps one way, and I'd hit the metal bed. Four or five the other way, and I'd smash into the barred door. Whatever was coming, I couldn't run away from it. Me, Benno, the fastest boy on the street, the boy who could outrun any policeman, the boy who never got caught. Until today. A groan started in my throat, but I swallowed it down.

The bear was moaning because she was scared, not because she was locked up. She'd been locked in a pen every night since she was a cub. Every morning I'd take her out. But here, in the cellar of the police station, in the cell next to mine, everything was strange to her. She didn't know if I would ever come. If I were with my bear, I would fold my arms around her thick neck, talk softly into her ear. But she was on the other side of the wall, where I couldn't touch her, couldn't even see her.

I knew what she was feeling. I'd felt that way with Papa. He used to tell me stories that his papa had told him. Once he told me that sometimes the earth starts to shiver, like a man dying of fever, making the houses rattle like teeth. The earth shakes harder and harder until it splits in two. And everything on the earth—houses, and people, and animals—all fall into the split and are swallowed up.

But Papa said that some of the animals know about this before it happens. The animals feel the shivering, deep down in the center of the earth, and they know that the earth is going to split apart, and they try to run away. Waiting there, in the stone cell, I could almost feel the shivering. I knew that a terrible thing was going to happen, but I couldn't run from it.

But maybe Papa could. I'd been the one they caught, not Papa. He hadn't broken the law. I had. If they let Papa go, they'd have to let my bear go, too. Then Papa could take my bear back home with him.

I knew Papa would be sure to feed her and clean her pen. And then I wouldn't feel so bad, even if I was locked up in this cell.

I wished my bear was with me.

I used to tell my bear a story. I'd tell her that there was a place where it was always summer. In that place, there was food everywhere. Wherever we walked, ripe fruit hung down from the trees—juicy apples, peaches, and oranges. If we whistled, bushels of nuts dropped down like soft rain. Mushrooms sprang up all over the ground, and none of them were poisonous.

There were lots of animals in that place, but there was no bear. And none of the animals was as strong or as smart as she was. My bear liked that part. Then I'd tell her that all the animals would guard us so that no one could hurt us ever again.

I told my bear that if we walked to the end of the city of Niestadt, and kept walking for a month and a day, we'd come to that place.

That night, I told myself the story, but I didn't stop where I always did, with my bear and me walking out of the city. This time I imagined the two of us walking, right past all the places we knew, to the very edge of the city, and then walking on—past places we'd never been. I couldn't even imagine what those places might be. I only saw the two of us—my bear and me—walking on and on, me in my boots, my bear on her big paws. I could hear my boots scuffing against the cobblestones, my bear's paws thumping.

But no, I wasn't hearing my bear's paws. I was hearing something else—two pairs of boots striking the stone floor in the hallway—one pair thudding, the other pair—Papa's hobnail boots—ringing against the stones. They hadn't let Papa go. Papa had been arrested because of what I'd done. Even if I could have run out of this cell, run the length of the city of Niestadt, run for a month and a day, I could never hide from Papa.

Please, I thought, please don't put him in this cell with me. Fear was rising in me like the flooding river.

The bear stopped moaning. She knew the sound of Papa's boots. She knew that if she moaned again, he'd take his stick to her. But my keeping silent wouldn't keep Papa's stick from me.

The footsteps stopped outside my cell. I looked toward the door. A grinning face appeared outside the bars—a face with waxy yellow skin and big horse teeth. It was the same policeman who'd locked me up. Had he come to take me out? Take the bear out?

The policeman unlocked the heavy door and, with both his arms, pulled Papa over and shoved him in with me. Then the door clanged shut, and the lock clicked behind us.

2

Quick In, Quicker Out

FOR A MOMENT Papa stood there, his legs apart, his broad body blocking the light from the hallway. Then he pushed past me as though I wasn't there. He didn't touch me, didn't even look at me. He dropped onto the bed and sat, his fists on his knees, staring at the opposite wall. His eyes burned through the half-dark.

The quiet shrieked and spun in my head. Papa knew that I'd gotten us caught—arrested—but he didn't know what I'd found. If he knew, then he'd be proud of me.

I tried to say *Papa*, but no sound came out. "Papa—" I tried again. My voice was a squeak. "Papa—the gentleman had a gold watch, real gold. I felt the hallmark."

In the dim cell, I couldn't see his eyes. Was he looking at me? I had to make him listen. The words burst out, loud and fast.

"Papa, I found the hallmark! The gentleman's watch. It had the hallmark."

Papa leaped to his feet, his head whipping first toward the hallway, where the policeman was sitting, then back to me. He raised his fists.

I ducked and tried to cover my head with my arms, but he pulled them down and shoved me into a corner. One of his hands wrapped around my arm and twisted it behind my back. I dropped to my knees, but I didn't cry out. I knew that would make Papa even angrier. The hurt in my arm would go away in a little while. But Papa's anger wouldn't go away for a long time. And his anger would hurt me much worse. I had to make him understand. If he understood, he wouldn't be angry.

"The man's purse," I said, my voice croaking. "Heavy with crowns. I felt a watch chain. A watch. Gold—the hallmark—crossed swords." Papa let go of my arm. Now that he knew, perhaps he wouldn't be so angry. "We would've been rich, Papa." The man's coat had been warm and had a soft fur collar. Me and Papa, we could have had warm coats, too. And warm, full bellies.

Papa lifted me to my feet and put his face close to mine. His red beard trembled. His breath was hot against my skin.

"What did I teach you, Benno? What did I teach you is the most important thing?"

"Quick in, quicker out, Papa."

"And were you out quick? No. You stood there, like a

clumsy, stupid sheep, and you felt for the watch, for the hallmark. What more did I teach you, Benno?"

My whole body was shivering. "You taught me to never stay in one place, always keep moving. I should have taken the purse and kept moving. I should have come back later for the watch." Why couldn't Papa understand? I only wanted to do good work, the best work I'd ever done.

Fast as a flame, Papa let go of my arm, and his big hand licked out and smacked me across my face, knocking me to the floor. Yes, Papa was right to hit me. All of us—my bear and Papa and me—were all locked up because of what I'd done, because I'd been so stupid. I stumbled to my feet. The rough stones had torn my trousers. I turned sideways so Papa wouldn't see the tear. Warm blood was trickling down my leg. My cheek stung.

"Papa—"

He shrugged me away. I was no more to him than a puff of air blowing through the cell.

I heard my bear blowing on the other side of the wall— quick, short breaths—and clacking her teeth, the way she did when she was afraid. When she was a cub, and she'd done something wrong, Papa would hit her with his stick. Very soon she grew afraid of Papa and his stick. My bear was never afraid of me, but this time, I could tell, she was afraid *for* me.

I could call to her, but Papa was right next to me, his anger hot as coals. If I called out to my bear, he'd hit me again. And that would make my bear even more afraid. I'd made a terrible mistake, and Papa was right to punish me, but my bear mustn't be frightened.

Out in the hallway, old Wax-Face was laughing like a whinnying horse. If Papa'd hit him, he wouldn't be laughing.

"You there, stop that!"

Wax-Face stopped laughing and stepped back. Another policeman with short gray hair and a long gray mustache unlocked the cell door and swung it open.

Papa turned away, his arms folded across his chest, his legs spread wide. I began to shiver.

The mustached policeman looked at Papa's icy back, opened his mouth as if to speak, but said nothing. Instead he led me out of the cell.

In the hallway, Mustache brought his face close to mine and took my chin in his hand. He smelled of lye soap. I jerked my head away and covered my bruised cheek. I didn't want any policeman looking at me.

"It's all right, son. I'll not beat you."

"If you ask me, a beating's what that boy needs," Wax-Face muttered from behind him.

Mustache whirled toward Wax-Face. "The only thing I'll be asking you is to keep your mouth shut. Your job is to sit there and watch and be quiet. I'm in charge of this boy."

I was worried about my bear. From the hallway, I could see through the bars of the door into her cell. She was backed into a corner, where the yellow light from the hallway barely reached, and she was rearing up, pawing the air and hurling her heavy head from side to side. The bear started to moan again, a faraway moan that dropped down low, then rose up high and dropped again.

I twisted and pulled, but I couldn't get free of the policeman.

"Calm down now, son. I don't know where to put you. We've only got two cells down here. I won't put you back with your papa, and the bear's in the other one."

I could see her, raking the air with her claws, baring her sharp teeth. Her white claws seemed to leap out of the darkness.

"Put me in there, put me in with my bear."

"I can't put you in that cell. She's wild. Look at those teeth, those claws. She could tear you to shreds."

"She's not wild. She's frightened, that's all. She's my bear, I take care of her. If I'm in there with her, she'll quiet down, I know she will."

Mustache's hands loosened a bit on my shoulders. I pulled away from him and ran to the door of my bear's cell. She lowered her front paws, her claws curving down toward the floor. But in the next second Mustache came up behind me and tried to drag me back. My bear reared up, warning him off with her claws and her teeth.

I held tight to the bars. "Get away!" I hissed at him. "You're scaring her."

He didn't move.

"Get away from me! Let me talk to her!"

"If she tries to hurt you—" Mustache stepped back.

"It's all right, Bear." I spoke to her as if I was humming, my voice coming low and soft. "You don't have to be afraid now, Bear. I'm here. No one's going to hurt you. No one'll hurt you now."

The bear swayed for a moment. Then her front paws whumped down on the stone floor. One heavy foot at a time, rolling her big head from side to side, she padded toward me. She was quiet, but her eyes kept jumping, from me to Mustache and back to me again.

"It's all right, Bear, it's all right."

Now she was close enough for me to reach through the bars and touch my fingertips to the short, spiky fur of her muzzle. She pressed the top of her head into my hands. Her warm breath and her meaty bear-smell filled me.

From behind me, Mustache reached out and unlocked the door of her cell.

I squeezed inside, and there she was, pushing her head against my chest. I put my arms around her heavy neck and pressed my mouth to the top of her head. Her rough fur tickled me. She twisted around, and her big tongue softly licked my face, melting away all the soreness in my cheek. I knelt down and rested my head against her shoulder, and there was only me and my bear, dark and warm and quiet.

"I'm going to bring you some supper." Mustache's voice burst the quiet, and my bear pulled back.

I stood up as he started down the hall. "Don't worry, Bear. I won't leave you." If they were going to keep us locked up, I'd make them lock us up together. But maybe they just wanted to scare us a little, and then they were going to let us go.

I called to Wax-Face, "Hey, how long are you going to keep us in here?"

"Oh, you'll be here a long, long time. You'll be growing a beard before you get out." He laughed his whinnying laugh, and his mouth curled into a grin around his horse teeth. I would have liked to throw something against those teeth and smash them in. He would never laugh at Papa.

Papa . . . For a while there'd been no sound from Papa's cell. But now through the wall I could hear his hobnail boots ringing the length of his cell—striking the stone floor, scraping as he turned.

The bear heard him, too, and stiffened. We both knew Papa had broken through his ice and was angry again. "It's not you, Bear, it's me he wants to beat," I told her. I put my arm around her neck and led her over to the bed. Tiredness was all through me. I sat down, and she lay on the floor at my feet. We were as far from Papa's cell as we could get, but our cell was small, and we could still hear the clang and scritch of his steps.

After a while Mustache came back. The bear slunk backward on her belly, her eyes turned up to me. Mustache unlocked the door and handed me a tray of food.

On the tray was a big plate of meat sandwiches and a couple of apples. My bear wanted the food. I could hear her guts grinding with hunger. But she wouldn't touch it. She knew that if she took food we hadn't given her—a fish from the market, a cabbage from a street vendor—Papa would put his stick to her.

The muscles in her back shivered. I picked up a sandwich and held it out to her. She stretched her head toward it.

"Eat it, Bear, it's for you. You can eat it."

She padded toward me, put her mouth into my hand, and whuffed it down.

I smelled the meat, felt the soft bread between my fingers. I didn't want to take some policeman's filthy food, I really didn't. But all winter long, there'd been no meat, no fresh bread. My belly wanted that food so badly it nearly leaped out of my mouth to grab it. Before I could stop myself, I was stuffing down a sandwich, eating it all. Then I was sorry. One at a time I fed the rest of the sandwiches and the two apples to my bear. She softly nuzzled the food from my hand and smacked her lips as she ate. When the food was gone, she licked the crumbs from the floor and from her muzzle.

We were alone now, me and my bear, but the sound of Papa's boots echoed through our cell—every clang saying *bad,* every scritch saying *stupid.* I couldn't stand the sound. I started to run, around and around the cell, my feet pounding against the stones. I wanted to run until the breath left my body. The cell was small, and I had to run in a tight circle, making my head run in circles, too. My bear began running beside me, her head bumping against my shoulder. She ran so close my legs got tangled up, and I fell across her back.

I sat on the floor and held on to her. I held her until the circles left my head, until we were dark and warm and quiet again. My bear lay down on her side. I sat beside her and stroked her head and watched her chest rising and falling as she went to sleep.

The pacing stopped in Papa's cell. I heard the metal bed creak. In the hallway, Wax-Face was snoring in his chair.

I took the blanket off the bed in my cell, spread it on the floor, and stretched out on half of it. My bear got up and lay down again, on the blanket, her belly against mine, one paw across my shoulder. In a moment she was asleep.

But I couldn't sleep. My sharp bones were fighting the stony floor. The thin blanket wasn't much help. Before long the dampness had seeped through, and I was sore and wet and cold. I lifted my chest onto my bear's side. Beneath her thick, rough coat, she was warm, and as she breathed, she rocked me up and down.

3

Papa

MY MAMA IS DEAD. She died before I could remember her. It was always the bear and me and Papa.

Papa was proud of his hands. He could make his fingers fly over the buttons of his concertina. Sometimes Papa's music made me feel like flying. In summer, after we'd had a good day, Papa would sit on his bed, his strong legs apart, playing his concertina, his fingers flitting across the buttons. When I was little, I'd flap around the room, dancing. "Look at me, Papa, I'm a bird." Papa would laugh and say that with my short legs, I looked like a crazy cockroach, running from the light.

Papa's hands were as big as skillets, and his fingers were as thick as sausages. But those thick fingers could twirl a potato against a knife blade as fast as the knife sharpener could twirl his wheel against a blade. And Papa could pare a potato or a turnip so thin that not a bit of the flesh stuck to the peel. That was good, because in winter potatoes and turnips were mostly what we had to eat. And bread. No sausages.

I couldn't peel potatoes or turnips like Papa. I'd peel away too much flesh, and Papa's face would get tight and he'd take the knife from me. And he didn't teach me to play the concertina. But Papa did teach me to do the work.

Papa taught me the way his papa had taught him. He put things into his pockets, buttons and dried beans, and he taught me to slide two fingers into his pockets and pull out what was there. If Papa felt my fingers in his pocket, his big hand would grab my fingers and squeeze them hard. Inside, I could feel myself being twisted and wrung, like a shirt on washday.

I learned fast. One day, when Papa was looking out the window, I reached into his pocket and pulled out all the coins in there. When I held out my hand and showed him what I'd gotten, he smiled widely. Then he sat down on his bed and pulled me onto his lap.

"When I was a boy," he said, "I lived in a village. I had three brothers and seven cousins and we were all taught to do the work. Well, one night, my cousin Simor—he was the oldest—he came home with his pockets full. He'd had a very good day, and he was feeling pretty pleased with himself. As Simor passed by our house, he saw me playing outside. He took out a copper and gave it to me and said, 'Here, go buy yourself a sweet.' Simor went straight home, but when he got there and reached into his pockets, they were empty. He knew I was the one who'd emptied them, and he came stomping over to our house, yelling that I'd stolen his whole day's work. I held out the copper and said, 'You gave me this and told me to buy myself a sweet, but I think you need it more than I do.' Then I knew that someday I would be the best.

"But from that day on . . ." Papa's face grew dark and he stopped speaking.

"What, Papa? What happened then?"

"Nothing happened. I knew that I was going to be the best, that's all."

I asked Papa what happened to Cousin Simor, to Papa's other cousins and his brothers. But Papa would not tell me the rest of the story, not then.

Papa was teaching me everything he knew about the work. He used to say, "Benno, you have fingers like a spider's legs. With those fingers, when I teach you, you will be even better at the work than I was." One spring day, when Papa was teaching me, I heard Pepi and Mohno and the other boys playing outside, calling and laughing. I wanted to be outside, running after the ball, laughing with them, the warm air rushing against my face. I reached for the beans in Papa's pocket as if I was reaching for the ball—with my whole hand and my fingers cupped.

Of course, my hand was clumsy, and Papa caught me. He grabbed my hand and held on to it.

"Benno, what are you doing?" he shouted. "This is not what I taught you."

"I'm sorry, Papa. I was thinking about the boys playing outside."

"Those boys? You want to be like them? Those useless boys with their worthless games? Go ahead, play with them. Become as useless as they are, playing all day long. Benno, you have good hands and you have a good head. You can learn the work. But the work is difficult. If you do not learn it well, someday you will make a terrible mistake."

Papa was quiet for a long time, looking out the window. Finally he turned back to me and said, "The mistake I made with Cousin Simor was a terrible one. After that it was all upside down."

I waited for him to go on.

When Papa spoke again, it was as if he was talking to himself. "I should not have taken the money from him. I shouldn't have shamed him. He never forgave me."

Papa fell silent. His face grew dark.

"Simor began to tell lies about me. When something bad happened—when a skunk drowned in the well, poisoning all the water, when our goat disappeared—Simor said I was to blame. Everyone in the family believed him. Cousin Simor was the best in the family, and I was only a boy. As I grew to be a man, Simor's lies grew worse. Then one night the family had a meeting. They decided that I must leave the village.

"Benno, a man's family is his blood. When he loses his blood, he dies.

"I left our village and I came here to the city. I was alone. Then, when I married your mother, I thought, We will have many children. Our blood will grow with our children. But your mother died." Papa pulled me to his chest. "Now I have only you, Benno."

Papa grew quiet again.

"You know, Benno," he said, "my papa had a bear. He trained it to dance so that people would come around to watch. Benno, we shall have a bear, too." Papa smacked his hand against his leg. "Yes! At the next fair, we shall buy a bear."

The bear was just a cub when Papa bought her from a trader who came over the mountains. Papa carried her home in a sack. The bear was frightened, and she clawed at the sack and screeched. But Papa was laughing all the while and telling me stories about his village. When we got to our room, Papa untied the end of the sack, lifted the cub out, and put her on the floor. She was small, even smaller than me, and as round as a melon. We both had ears that stuck out, mine on the sides of my head and the bear's on top of hers. Her fur was dark brown like my hair, and soft, but her eyes were even softer.

The bear didn't move. She just sat where Papa put her, screeching softly, showing her little white teeth. I reached out my hand and touched her head with the tips of my fingers. I was afraid she would bite me with those sharp teeth, but she didn't. She rolled her head to one side so that I could scratch behind her small round ear, and then she waddled into my lap. I put my arms around her neck and pressed my lips onto the flat place on top of her head.

That night, when I lay down to sleep on my mat, she crawled onto my chest. She was warm. I remembered once when I'd been sick, so clattering cold with fever that even the blanket from Papa's bed couldn't stop my shivers, Papa had warmed a brick on top of the stove. Then he'd wrapped the brick in rags and put it on my chest. The bear was warm like that. She pushed against my chest, first with one fat paw and then with the other—her paw pads were pink—and made a chuffing noise deep in her throat. Her claws were sharp, but the chuffing noise was soft. After a while she stopped pushing, and then I pressed my lips onto the flat place on her head, and I whispered, "Good night, Bear."

The next day, Papa bought goat's milk, eggs, ground oats, and honey for the bear and me.

"The cub must have good food," he said, "so that she will grow strong."

He bought a tube from the apothecary. When we got home, he mixed a yellow pap from the milk, eggs, honey, and oats. He filled the tube with the pap and put one end into his mouth and the other into the cub's. She grabbed the tube in her paws, and while Papa blew into the tube, she sucked down the pap.

"Papa, let me. I want to feed her."

"You must be careful. When she takes the tube in her mouth, blow into it, but slowly, not too fast."

I blew too fast. Yellow drops sprayed over her face.

Papa reached for the tube, but I held on to it. "I can do it. I'll do it right this time."

"Don't waste the food, Benno. It's costing us good money. If you can't do it right, I will feed her."

I blew softly, and from then on, I was the one who fed the cub. While she sucked, she used to dig her sharp claws into my chest.

"Papa, her claws are hurting me. Why does she do that?"

"She thinks you're her mama," he said, "giving her milk."

That first spring, she was too little to work, and so was I. But we put her on a rope, and she scampered with Papa and me into the city. We stood by him while he worked. Papa would play lively tunes, and I would hold the rope while the little bear made fat circles around me. When people saw the bear and me, they stopped and smiled. Some of them tickled the bear and gave me coins. Then Papa would take off his hat, bow, say, "Thank you most kindly," and take more coins out of their pockets.

The bear grew fast. When summer came, Papa said it was time to start training her. He'd take a piece of fruit in his hand and hold it up high, over the cub's head. When she stood up on her hind legs to grab the fruit with her paws, he let her get it. But when she tried to put her front paws down again, he took his stick and struck her across her shoulders. When the cub tried to grab Papa's stick in her teeth, he kicked her with his heavy boots. She screamed, *uh-waaa, uh-waaa,* high and shrill, and dropped the stick. I closed my eyes and covered my ears, but I could still hear her screaming.

"Papa, don't hit her! You're hurting her."

"Be still, Benno. You don't know what you're talking about. In my papa's day, they taught the bears to dance by putting hot trays beneath their feet, so they would dance from one foot to the other. Stop that crying or I'll give *you* something to cry about."

The bear learned, when Papa picked up his stick, to stand up and not put her front paws down again. And she learned, too, when Papa began to play his concertina, to pick up one foot and then the other, to turn herself around, so that it looked like she was dancing.

By the end of the summer, the bear had grown so large that our room was too small for her to dance in. The first time Papa took the bear down to the courtyard, the boys stopped playing ball and the old men put down their cards. They all wandered over to watch. Papa let them stay, but if they came too close, he warned them off with his stick.

When Papa sent me to the pump to get some water for the bear, my friend Pepi followed me. Mohno dragged behind him.

"Benno, could I touch your bear?" Pepi asked. "I won't hurt her."

"No, you can't. I'd let you, but my papa doesn't let anyone touch her but me. I feed her and she sleeps with me."

"Aah," Mohno snarled. "Who believes you? I bet she'll bite your hand off, the way she bites the stick."

"She'd bite you, Mohno, if I told her to."

"Come on, Pepi," Mohno muttered. "I've got something to show you. It's better than that old bear." And he led Pepi away.

Whenever me and Papa went to buy the goat's milk, we left the bear in our room. Papa would tell the dairyman the milk was for his little boy, and I would smile as sweet as I could, and then the dairyman would put a little extra into the milk can. One day, when we came back to our room, pots were toppled off the stove and barley covered the floor. The cupboard door hung open, and the potatoes, carrots, beets, and the whole cone of sugar were gone. The bear was sitting on her haunches in the middle of the floor, licking her paws. She'd eaten everything but the barley. I thought Papa was going to beat the bear, but he didn't.

Papa knew what I was thinking. "If I beat her now, Benno, it will mean nothing. She ate the food while we were gone. That was the time to teach her. If I beat her now, she won't know why."

He told me to sweep up all the barley, dig it out of the cracks between the floorboards, and put it into a sack. Then he went down to the courtyard to build the bear a wooden pen.

Papa made the pen out of tall boards, with strong posts in the corners. He nailed the boards tightly together, with no spaces between. He said he didn't want people jabbing the bear or throwing things at her. At one end, he fixed a canvas over the top, to keep the rain and snow off the bear. But he left the other end open, to let the light in. Opposite the canvas end, he put in a strong door and fastened it with a lock.

When Papa first put the bear into the pen, she poked her black nose into every corner, sniffing. Then she stood up and tried to see over the boards, but they were much too tall.

I followed her into the pen. "Bear, this is where you'll be sleeping from now on. See, there's straw over here in the corner—that'll be your bed."

"Benno, come out of there now."

Papa led me out and locked the door of the pen behind us. I heard her crying, *uh-waaaah, uh-waaaah, uh-waaaah*—a sound like a blade cutting through iron. I pulled away from Papa and pressed my eye against a small hole in one of the boards. The bear was sitting up, her front paws hanging between her back legs, the cries ripped from deep inside her.

"Papa, she's crying, she's frightened. Let me go back in and talk to her. She'll be quiet if I talk to her."

"Let her be, Benno. She must learn to stay in the pen."

"But Papa—"

Papa pulled me away. "She will cry tonight. And she will cry tomorrow night and maybe the night after that. But she will learn that crying will do her no good, and she will stop."

Papa put his big hand against my back and shoved me toward the stairs. At the top, I tried to twist around and look down through the opening into the bear's pen, but Papa opened the door and pushed me through. Until it shut behind us, I could hear her crying.

That night I lay on my mat and I cried, too. But I didn't make a sound. I tried to think about good things. I thought about the times in summer when it rained for days and days, and we couldn't work in the city. Then Papa would say, "Today, Benno, we will go to the woods for our food." We couldn't take the bear to the woods. Papa said if we took her, she'd remember where she came from and go wild. She'd never again stay in a pen or be led on a chain or dance. So I'd hug my bear good-bye and whisper in her ear that there'd be a good supper for her when we came back.

We took the horse trolley. There were long wooden benches down both sides of the car. Papa and I sat in the middle of one. When other people got on, they looked at us and then they sat on the other side or far down at the ends. Papa didn't look at them. He just stared straight ahead as though we were the only people in the car. We took the trolley to where it stopped at a dirt road, and then we walked until the dirt road became a path and then there was no path, only the woods.

I loved the smells—the sharp, clean smell of the pine trees, the dark, cloudy smell of the damp earth. I filled my whole body with those smells. And under the trees, in the brown earth, and on top of rotting logs, we found mushrooms. If my bear had been with me, I could have stayed in the woods forever.

Papa seemed bigger in the woods, taller. He filled his chest with long, deep breaths, and he took long, deep steps. When Papa found a patch of mushrooms, he would spread a cloth on the ground and slice the mushrooms free with his knife, turning each mushroom over in his thick fingers, then tossing it onto the cloth.

"Look up, Benno, what do you see?"

"I see pine trees, Papa."

"Now look down. See, this mushroom grows under pine trees, and its flesh is as sweet as the smell of the pines. See how white the stem is, Benno. But remember, if the stem is not white, if it looks red or yellow, do not take it, it is poisonous. You must never make a mistake with a mushroom, Benno. With a mushroom, you only get one mistake."

We walked all over the woods. Papa would show me the mushrooms that grow under the white birch trees and the ones that grow on the edge of the woods. And he would show me the mushrooms that we must never pick. Papa knew all about mushrooms. He knew everything, and he was going to teach me so I would know everything, too.

At the end of the day, we would bundle up the cloth with the mushrooms inside. On the trolley, I held the bundle on my lap. Our hands and our clothes were soaked in the deep, dark smell of them.

Back in our room, Papa would cook the mushrooms with onions until they made a thick, brown stew. I'd heap the bear's basin with the stew and carry it down to her. "Didn't I tell you, Bear," I'd say, "there'd be a good supper?" She'd smack and grunt and lick every drop of the mushroom gravy from her basin. Then I'd go back upstairs and me and Papa would eat until our bellies ached.

I learned a lot from Papa. And I learned from Old Man Rumitch. Old Man Rumitch had a room on the floor below us. When we had something to sell, we knocked on his door. The locks scraped and clanked as Old Man Rumitch opened them. Then a crack of light would show at the edge of the door, and he'd peer at us over a chain. When he saw it was us, he'd unfasten the chain and let us in.

The biggest thing in the whole room was a tall, black cabinet nearly as high as the ceiling. It stood on feet shaped like animal paws—carved paws with fur and toes and claws. I used to wonder if maybe, at night, the cabinet stood up on its furry paws and walked around. I imagined it walking like my bear, on stiff legs, with its feet flat. The cabinet had more doors than I could count, and each door had a lock.

When we brought Rumitch something very good, he would open the tall black cabinet and take out a tin and give me a sweet. Then he would put back the tin, take out a bottle, and pour a splash from it into two glasses. I sucked my sweet slowly, but Papa and Rumitch drank from their glasses in one gulp. While the candle burned down they sat and talked and told stories about the old times.

I liked hearing them talk. Papa didn't talk to the people who lived in our court, or the people in the shops where we sometimes bought things. "You see how they are with us, Benno, they see us and they move away."

Like the people who wouldn't sit near us on the trolley.

"They think that if they keep their distance, they will be safe from us. Let them stay away, they will never be safe. We are smarter than they are—smarter, quicker, and cleverer. But Rumitch," Papa said, "Rumitch is one of us."

Once we brought Rumitch a gold watch. He snorted and held out his hand for it. He stared at the watch with his watery eyes.

"Eh, who took this watch?"

"Benno did. He has good hands, fingers like a spider's legs." Papa's eyes flashed in the candlelight. "And he's smart, Rumitch, very smart."

Gladness poured all through me.

"Yes, Benno, you have good hands. But the hands know only what they touch. Good hands are not enough, you must also have good eyes, Benno. The hands do not know everything. This watch, it is gold on the outside, but on the inside, pheh! Come here."

Old Man Rumitch went to the cabinet. Not for a sweet. The watch wasn't good enough. There wouldn't be any splashing drinks or stories tonight. He unlocked one of the small doors, pulled open a drawer behind it, and took out another gold pocket watch.

"Look at this watch, Benno. Look at it carefully. What do you see?"

The front of the watch looked the same as the watch I had taken—a circle of gold, a stem at one end attached to a gold chain, a round white face with numbers in a circle, two lacy, golden hands. But then I turned it over. On the back was a little carving of two crossed swords.

"That's right, Benno. That is the hallmark, the mark of solid gold. Remember what it looks like."

I ran my fingers lightly over the back of the watch. I felt the cool, flat gold and the tiny hollow that was the hallmark. My fingers traced the edges of the hollow. They would remember the hallmark, the sign of solid gold.

Papa saw my fingers on the hallmark. And Papa said, "Rumitch, Benno's fingers are his eyes. His fingers will not forget."

I didn't forget what Old Man Rumitch taught me. But today in the market, today, I forgot what Papa taught me.

4

The Stalls

WHEN I WOKE UP THAT MORNING, the sky outside the window of our room was lightening to gray. There was ice on the windowpanes and on the sill. During the night, the coal in the stove had all burned down.

Out in the dark, crooked hallway, the air was as thick as cooked lentils and stank of cabbage, fish heads, and oily smoke. I always held my breath until I reached the outside door.

The iron stairs leading down to the courtyard were slick with ice, but I wasn't worried—I was surefooted anywhere.

All I was thinking about was my bear, waiting for me in her pen. It was the same every morning. When I looked into her pen from the top of the stairs, she would be standing on her hind legs, stretching her head up to me, the muscles in her shoulders trembling with excitement. It wasn't because she heard me coming. Even if I opened and closed the door without a sound, when I looked down, she would be there, standing very still, as if she'd been that way for a while. I think she just knew I was coming, the way she always knew everything about me.

That morning, the lock on her pen was frozen and the key wouldn't turn. I had to light a match under the lock to warm it, but my bear didn't want to wait. She'd gotten down on all fours and was clawing the boards on the inside of her pen. There were deep ruts where she'd clawed, wanting me to open the door and be with her. "You've got to wait a bit, Bear. The lock's still frozen and I can't open it yet."

When she heard the key turn, she stopped. I squeezed around the door and leaned it shut behind me. My bear wasn't the only one who knew what was going to happen. In a second she was pushing one paw against my chest with all of her weight. If I hadn't had the door behind me, she would have knocked me over. "Take it easy, Bear, you're not a little cub anymore." She put her paw down, laid her big head against mine, and tickled her scratchy muzzle across my cheek. Then she lowered her head and sniffed at my pockets.

I pulled out a potato and a turnip and held them out to her, one in each hand. "I was going to give these to you after your breakfast, but you were too smart for me. I can't fool you, can I, Bear." Last night I'd saved them for her from my supper. I don't much like turnips, but I'd really wanted that potato. Her warm tongue licked lightly against my cold hands.

I opened the door a crack to get her food basin. Her breakfast that winter wasn't much—a loaf of stale bread, some wrinkled apples, potato and turnip peels, brown and soft like the apples. She lowered her head into the basin and ate, smacking her lips and huffing. When she finished, she licked the empty basin for the last crumbs.

I carried it to the water pump, which sat in the middle of a pool of ice. The handle was frozen hard. I had to tug with all my strength to break it free.

There was still the bear's pen to clean. With a rusty shovel, I turned over the straw she slept on. Some of the straw at the bottom was a little moldy, but I pulled it out and pushed the rest together. The straw would last a few days more. My bear stood beside me, watching.

In a corner, away from her straw bed, were her droppings. She never dirtied the rest of her pen—just the one spot, as if that was her slop bucket. We never even had to teach her to do that. When she was little and stayed in our room, she picked one corner for her droppings. Papa found newspapers on the street and put them there, and she never dirtied anywhere else. I don't know if all bears are like that. I don't think so. I shoveled up her frozen droppings, covered them with the moldy straw, and carried the shovel out to the street. There were piles of garbage and horse droppings on both sides. The horses weren't like my bear—they left their droppings wherever they stood. Maybe other bears did, too.

My bear didn't just like her pen kept clean, she liked to be kept clean herself. I combed her every morning, starting at her head and working my way back down, picking out the pieces of straw that stuck to her fur. Her fur had become light brown, like the color of dry, dusty earth. The hair around her muzzle and eyes was short and scratchy. Her cheek fur was longer and thicker, but along her back there were patches where her fur had fallen out and her pale skin showed through. The muscles in her shoulders and haunches were like heavy ropes, but her bones stuck up all along her back, like the teeth of the iron comb. If I combed over those bones, she shied away from me, so I was careful not to touch them.

"I know, Bear, you've gotten skinny this winter. But next summer, you'll see, the work'll go better and you'll have plenty to eat." The bear's ears were like furry spoons, and they scooped the air for every sound, following me as I moved around her.

It was still early. I hunkered down on her straw, and she settled herself next to me. I scratched behind her ears. She rolled her head from side to side, her eyes half-closed, and grunted and hummed. Then I slid my hands down and scratched under her chin. "You like that, don't you, Bear. You think I can sit here all day long, scratching you. You wouldn't care if we never went to work, would you."

From down in her pen, I could see only the top floor of the Stalls, where we live. People call it the Stalls because the courtyard used to be a horse market, with the horses kept in stone stalls around it. The rim of the sun crept over the rooftops. Pigeons flew up from under the eaves, cooing. I leaned against my bear's back, and we were quiet, listening to the pigeons.

The sun was higher and brighter when the bear tensed and got to her feet. Papa was standing at the top of the stairs, his concertina hanging from his hand. The sun lit up Papa's red hair, turning it to fire. "Time to start, Benno."

I hooked the chain onto her leather collar and led her into the courtyard. Pepi and Mohno were starting for school, with their book bags and lunch buckets. I felt sorry for them, having to go to school. Well, I felt sorry for Pepi anyway. I waved my free hand at them.

Mohno pretended he didn't see me and my bear. Pepi waved back and twisted his mouth into a sort of smile. I knew Pepi wished he could have been me, free as the river. Most of all, Pepi wished he had a bear. All the boys did. I was the only boy in the Stalls, maybe the only boy in the whole city of Niestadt, who had a bear. Once, Pepi caught a mouse and taught it to do tricks. The mouse used to eat out of his hand, run up his sleeve, and climb out onto Pepi's head.

Then Mohno got a dog. He said his dog caught rats and that it could eat Pepi's mouse in one gulp. But when I got the bear, even Mohno stopped bragging.

I knew Papa didn't like me to play with the other boys. "They are not our blood, Benno," he'd say. "They are not like us."

Anyway, in the winter, I couldn't play outside. When me and Papa came home at night, it was already dark and cold, and everyone kept inside.

But on summer nights, I waited until Papa lay down on his bed, sweat slicking his forehead and eyelids. Then I'd say, "Papa, I'm going down to be with my bear. It's cooler outside." And I'd take my bear out of her pen. Even while I was opening the lock, I could hear her prancing paws bouncing off the packed earth. I didn't need to lead her out, she led me. I had to run hard to keep up with her.

Right through the courtyard she pulled me, my arm that held her chain stretched straight out, my legs scudding. All day my bear'd been waiting for this. Out in the street, the boys were shouting, laughing, running. She heard them and she wanted to run with them. Not really with them, ahead of them. I was faster than any other boy, but my bear was even faster. If I hadn't been holding her chain, she would have been out of sight in a moment. No, that's not true. Even if I hadn't held her chain, she never would have run away from me. I could feel the power in her body as she ran, hear the pounding of her heavy paws churning up clouds of dust. But even so, I could tell she was holding back, slowing herself to stay with me.

My bear and me ran and ran in the street, the other boys running and yelling behind us, until I was sweating and tired and dropped to the ground. My bear stopped with me, but still she wanted to run. She hopped from one leg to the other, circling around me, begging me to get up and run some more. "I can't, Bear," I panted. "It's too hot."

Then one of the boys would say, "Can I ride on your bear?" And I'd say all right. When a boy came up to my bear, she'd stand very still and look around, all peaceful, as if she didn't even know he was there. But she knew. She'd wait while the boy climbed on her back and grabbed onto her neck. And then she'd rear up tall, twist around, and toss him off just as if he was a piece of straw. Everybody knew she'd do that, but they wanted to try to ride her anyway.

Once Mohno said, "Aah, none of you can ride her. But I can wrestle that bear, I bet." He tried to grab her around her neck, but she pushed him over and sat on him until he was choking and gasping. She didn't like Mohno.

"That's enough, Bear. Get up," I said. She got off Mohno, sat down on her haunches, and looked all peaceful again.

But now it wasn't a summer night, it was a winter morning, and my bear and me were going to work. I knew Mohno was watching. He pretended not to see me, looking toward the window of his room like his mother was calling to him.

"Come on, Bear," I said loudly. "We can't be wasting time this morning." I put my arm across my bear's shoulders and walked with my head up behind Papa, through the courtyard and out the gate.

The street was all ragged holes filled with icy water. Me, I was jumping over the smaller holes and hopping to the sides of the bigger ones. But the bear just walked straight on, with her front toes pointing in and her head swinging from side to side. She stepped right into the holes. The fur on her legs was still long and thick. I'd combed it so she'd look nice, but now it was all stiffened into muddy points. She was splashing me, too, and my breeches were wet and cold.

On both sides of the street, the tilting wooden houses cracked and shivered. In the dark alleys between the houses, cats, thin as string, prowled for mice and rats and clawed at the piles of frozen garbage. When they saw the bear, they hissed at her. She turned her head toward the alleys, sniffing the air. Then she looked back at me, her eyes begging. It wasn't the snarling cats she wanted, it was the frozen garbage. She wanted me to say to her, Go ahead, Bear, claw through the ice, find the food, fill your belly. But I kept walking, past the alleys, and my bear did, too, leaving the prints of her paw pads and her hooked claws in the mud.

The streets were all mud in the Lowlands District where we lived. When we got to the River Resier, we walked along the bank. Even early in the morning, the river was awake. There were boats and barges and paddle steamers churning the icy water. One of the boatmen waved at us.

An old boatman used to live in the Stalls. Once he told me that boys no bigger than me went to sea on ships. They sailed down the River Resier, out of the city of Niestadt, right out of the country. He told me that the Resier joined an even bigger river, the Danube, and that river flowed through great cities, much greater than our city of Niestadt, until it flowed into a great sea, the Black Sea. And from there, the boys sailed all over the world, and they saw very strange, very grand sights. He said they saw men who wore gowns and women who wore trousers, houses that stood on stilts, and wagons pulled by people instead of horses. He said they saw animals as big as horse trolleys and plants that ate animals. I asked, if I went on one of those ships, could I take my bear? He said he'd never heard of any animals on ships, except for cats, which they kept to catch rats. I would have liked to sail on a ship like that and see those sights, but I couldn't leave my bear behind.

Near the stalls, there used to be a bridge over the river. But every spring, the River Resier flooded. One year the river washed out the bridge. They never put it back up again. So Papa and me and the bear walked along the river and crossed over on the Middle Bridge.

The pavement on the bridge was dry, but it was hard to walk there. The bridge was crammed with carts and drays and horse-drawn wagons and carriages. The walkways on both sides were jammed with people. From the top of the bridge I could see the tall buildings of brick and stone on the other side, with lacy towers and domes that glittered in the sun.

We came to a broad avenue with fancy shops and sidewalks that were swept dry, but we still walked in the street. If we walked on the sidewalk, the ladies would pull their skirts away and the gentlemen would shake their sticks at us. Their boots never got wet. But mine did. This morning, my toes felt as if someone was hammering thin, sharp nails into them.

The sun was higher now. Papa put his arm across my shoulder. "The sun is shining, Benno. Today will be a good day."

5

The Market

ODAY WE WERE GOING to the Central Market.
There were many markets in the city—the horse
market, the iron market, the flower market in summer—
but the Central Market was the biggest of all. Every day,
we worked in a different place so that people wouldn't
remember us. My boots were wet, my hands and feet
were freezing, but I didn't care anymore. My bear and
me, we didn't feel right in the tight shells of rooms and
pens, in the shut-in streets. It was better in summer, when
my feet were bare and my hands were warm. But today I
knew my feet, my fingers, even in the cold, would be as
light as moths.

The Central Market was in a big open square, with
shops on all four sides, their windows dripping steam.
We walked past the meat and poultry sellers, with their
crates of squawking chickens and geese and slabs of meat

hanging from hooks overhead. Women were holding up chickens and blowing on their feathers to look at the flesh underneath. They were pinching the slabs of meat to make sure they were fresh.

In the middle of the square, lines of wooden tables were heaped with thick woolen sweaters and leather boots, trays of silvery fish, mountains of green apples, orange carrots, and purple beets.

Rich ladies didn't shop in the market. They sent their cooks. The cooks strutted about as if they were fine ladies themselves and called out loudly what Madam would like today. They were as plump as pigeons and their chins wobbled. Their little cloth purses were fat, too.

Sometimes rich gentlemen strolled through the market. And sometimes they stopped and plucked out bright red apples with their fingertips. They paid for the apples with coins that they took from fine leather purses that gleamed like chestnuts. They sliced the apples with little silver pocketknives and ate the slices as they strolled. Once, I found one of those silver knives—a gentleman must have dropped it. I kept it and never told Papa, or he would have sold it.

I walked quickly past the market stalls, my belly in knots. One time when I was little, I took an apple from a stand. Papa saw me do it, and he pulled me by my ear and made me give the apple back. He smacked me and told me never to do it again. I wanted to know why I couldn't take the apple. Papa snarled, "The vendors are all cheats and thieves, every one of them, but if we steal anything from them, they'll call the police on us." Even when I was little, I was afraid of the police. I never took another apple from the market.

My bear didn't take anything either. Her big black nose twitched when we passed the piles of apples and carrots. I had to pull hard on her chain when we walked by the trays of fish. But she never took a thing.

We shouldered our way through the crowd—women carrying baskets and net bags, men pushing handcarts heaped with clothes and shoes, wheelbarrows full of potatoes and turnips—until we came to an open place. Papa took the bear's chain from me and wrapped it around his wrist.

"Benno," he said in a low voice. I came closer. "The market is crowded today, filled with fools. But don't you be a fool. Keep your wits about you, Benno, keep your wits. And, Benno," he added, "watch for my signals."

"I will, Papa." Today Papa would be proud of me.

Papa stretched out his concertina and started to play a marching tune. Papa's arms opened and closed, his feet tapped in time to the music, and his mouth behind the red beard spread into a smile.

As soon as she heard the music, the bear lifted her head and looked at me.

"Go ahead, Bear," I whispered. "Dance."

The bear stood up on her hind legs and began to sway and twist. A thick circle of people gathered around, pointing at the dancing bear and laughing.

I laughed, too—at them. I was going to empty their pockets. When we went home that night, their pockets would be light and my pockets would be heavy. I'd turn out my pockets onto the table in our room and spread out all the coins, maybe even some bracelets and such that Old Man Rumitch would give us money for. And then Papa would send me out to the shops, and I'd fill our basket with bread—fresh, soft bread, spicy sausages, sweet-smelling tea, and tart, juicy oranges. I could already smell the sausages crackling on the stove, feel the juice of the oranges spraying my face as I pulled them apart. Then my bear would eat until her belly was round. And me and Papa, we'd laugh about all the fools we'd seen.

But that would be later. First I had to look them all over. Every crowd was different, and I had to find the easiest ones, the ones with the fattest purses. I walked up to a young mother with a baby in her arms, took off my cap, and shone my smile at her. She dropped a copper in my cap. Next to her was an old woman. I made myself very small and thin, even smaller and thinner than I am. "Please, Missus, it's been a long winter, and I have been very hungry." Three coppers in the cap.

I put the coppers into my pocket so that the cap would look empty. People didn't give me any coppers when they saw I already had some. But I wanted more than coppers. When people took out their purses, I was looking where those purses came from, and I was looking for the fat purses, the heavy ones.

My eyes were everywhere. And my ears. I heard Papa's concertina, saw my bear, tall, turning. And I saw Papa watching me. He closed his lips tightly together, saying to me, Not yet, keep looking. I kept looking. Not that woman, not the fat one without a bonnet and smelling of grease. She'd been standing at her stove when she saw she needed an egg or a sausage for her husband's supper. She'd pulled on a shawl right over her apron and run out to the market. She wouldn't have brought much money, just enough to buy what she needed.

Not that cobbler, either, in the leather apron, the one with little black squirrel eyes. He'd just stopped to listen to the music. All of his money was back in his shop, in a drawer under the counter.

But that woman with the freckled hands, fussily picking over the potatoes. She had two marketing baskets hanging loosely from her arm. She was going to buy a lot, two baskets' worth, but she hadn't bought anything yet. When she'd filled her baskets, she'd be holding one in each hand, and they'd be heavy, pulling her arms straight down. But now her baskets were empty and her purse full. I looked at Papa, playing, tapping, smiling. He blinked his eyes. As lightly as a feather falling from a pigeon, my hand dipped into one of the baskets and came out with her purse. She never looked up from the potatoes.

And then they came strutting up, the fighting cocks. That's what I called that bunch of young fellows who came to the market with their chests puffed out, jabbing each other with their fists and elbows. They sized up the bear out of the ends of their eyes.

Papa saw them, too. He stopped playing his concertina. Now it was my turn to be heard. I walked up to one of them, a big fellow with a nose like a turnip and his hat pushed to the back of his head. I grinned and said, "You're a pretty big fellow. Strong, too, I bet. Think you could wrestle that bear?" I said the same thing every time they came. Just as though he didn't wrestle my bear every time he came. Just as though she didn't win every time. The other fellows started slapping Turnip-Nose on the back and pushing him forward.

"Yeah, sure. I can wrestle him easy. What's in it for me if I win?"

I began to run through the marketplace, shouting, "A man is going to wrestle the bear. Come and watch. Bear wrestling. Come quick." From all directions, people rushed over. I held out my cap again, but this time I said, really loud, "Place a bet—if the big fellow wins, we'll double your money. Place a bet on the big fellow." People were shoving to get closer, elbowing each other to drop their coins into the cap. Now the more coins there were in my cap, the more coins people wanted to throw in.

They were getting excited just watching the winnings grow.

"What are his chances?" a man was asking one of the fighting cocks. "Think he can win?"

"Of course he can. He never loses."

"Oh, yeah?" A young fellow with a sooty face, pushing a wheelbarrow full of coal, shouted out, "Tell you what. After he loses to that bear, he can take me on."

Turnip-Nose took off his hat and handed it to one of his friends. Then he took off his jacket, folded it carefully, and placed it over his hat. He opened his shirt collar, rolled up his sleeves, and with his knees and elbows spread apart, he strutted in a circle around the bear.

I put my cap on the ground at Papa's feet. I wasn't going to need it now. The real work was about to begin.

Papa put down his concertina and let go of the bear's chain. Turnip-Nose ran at the bear. She stood up as tall as his head, and he grabbed her around the middle. Papa did the talking now. Half singing, he was calling out to Turnip-Nose, "That's the way. Hang on tight now. A bear's no match for a man like you."

Then softly, so only Turnip-Nose could hear: "There's a pretty young thing over there, watching. I don't think it's the bear she's looking at."

Then loudly again: "Thank you, sir, for your bet. And you, too, kind gentleman."

Papa always said, "You can't take a man's money if he's looking at you." So the bear was our look-away.

While she was wrestling, everyone was looking at her, pushing and shoving to get closer. No one was looking at me, no one felt my fingers.

I slithered through the crowd, always keeping behind, keeping low, looking for the pocket that had the heavy purse, the wrist that had the bracelet. That man over there, the one with the face like a shriveled apple, where would he keep his money? From the looks of him, he kept it close to his heart. He blew his nose into a handkerchief, using his right hand. Now I was certain his purse would be inside his coat on the left, where his heart was. While old Apple-Face wiped his nose, I swiped his purse. A fat one.

Six purses, a bracelet, even a locket. Oh, what a supper we were going to have tonight!

The bear had her front paws wrapped around Turnip-Nose, and he couldn't move. Papa began to play again and the bear started dancing, lifting Turnip-Nose right off the ground. No one laughed at the bear now. She was stronger than the strongest man in the market.

The bear started rolling on the ground, over and over, still holding on to the big fellow. When she stopped, she sat right down on top of him, her legs on either side of his chest, waving her long claws in the air. She thought she was playing, just like with Mohno. Maybe she thought I was going to come running back and tell her to get up. But I couldn't do that, not yet. The bear had Turnip-Nose pinned to the ground, and he couldn't break free. The crowd was yelling that the bear had won.

Just then a gentleman came strolling up, a gentleman wearing a thick gray overcoat with a fur collar. I slid my fingers inside his overcoat. This wasn't easy—he was wearing a silk scarf and my fingers got tangled in the fringe. And under the scarf, he was wearing a jacket and a waistcoat. I very slowly worked my fingers inside his jacket. The cloth of his suit was fine. I felt for his purse. Through the soft leather, I could feel the heavy crowns. I placed my two fingers around the purse and plucked it out.

As I brought my fingers out, they brushed against a watch chain. I knew that the watch would be solid gold. It had to be.

In my mind, I could hear Papa's voice saying, "Quick in, quicker out." But if the watch was gold . . . I'd put it into Papa's hand and his eyes would grow bright. I could hear Rumitch clucking over the watch, taste the sweet melting in my mouth, hear the splashing drinks and the laughing stories.

I could see my bear, flopping down on her straw, her belly full, making the chuffing sound deep in her throat, the sound she made when she was a cub and happy.

Quick in, quicker out. I knew that. But this one time I needed an extra few seconds. I put the purse into my own pocket and reached back under the coat, under the jacket, to the waistcoat, and followed the chain to the watch. My fingers were trembling as I ran them over the back of the watch. It was there, the hallmark!

Suddenly a strong hand grabbed my wrist.

I kicked out hard, and the man cursed and let go. I took off.

"Stop, thief! Stop that boy, he's a thief!"

I snaked through the crowd, faster and smaller than I'd ever been in my life.

Someone in the crowd began shrieking, "That boy was taking bets on the bear. He's working for the old man. They're both thieves together. Get them!"

"Get the old man!"

"Grab the bear's chain!"

I started to run down a street on one side of the market. My bear! I couldn't run away and leave her. I stopped and looked back. The crowd was like the river in a storm, waves of them, rushing against Papa and the bear, beating at them with fists and sticks. "Run, Bear, run!" I called to her. At the sound of my voice, the bear began to rear up on her hind legs, wanting to look for me.

Papa was fighting back. But Papa had trained the bear well, trained her not to fight the stick. She just dropped her head and let them beat her.

6

Mister Magistrate Hookim

O UTSIDE THE POLICE STATION, it was snowing again.
Winter had never left. Mustache was in front of us,
then came Papa, then me and my bear, and then another
policeman behind us.

"Where are you taking us?" I called to Mustache.

"You've got to appear before the magistrate," he called
back.

I felt sick. Papa'd told me about magistrates. They
were worse than policemen. If you kept a sharp eye, you
could dodge a policeman. But you couldn't dodge a magistrate. Once you went before a magistrate, you were
finished, locked up, gone.

I looked at my bear. Her leg fur was still all muddy
points from walking through the puddles. I wished I had
her comb to make her look nice. I wished it was yesterday, with the sun just coming up and the pigeons cooing,

and Papa not yet awake. I wished I'd never gone back in for that watch.

But wishing wouldn't change anything. It wouldn't change what I'd done, it wouldn't change what the magistrate was going to do to us. And it wouldn't change what Papa would do.

The courthouse was a great white building, with high steps and two enormous black doors. They led us down hallway after hallway into a room with dark green walls. On the side walls were two lines of dark pictures with bright, golden frames. Like the watch. Sitting on benches on both sides of the room were the people from the market.

They were all cleaned up and dressed in their Sunday clothes. The fat woman was wearing a flowered shawl instead of her greasy apron, and the coal carter had scrubbed his sooty face until it was pink. Turnip-Nose had put something slick on his hair, so it was as shiny as a fish. If I hadn't been so good at studying faces, I wouldn't have recognized any of them. Only the man with the shriveled-apple face looked the same, but this time he was making sure to keep his hand inside his coat, where he kept his purse.

When the two policemen led us in, the people elbowed each other and pointed. My bear saw them, and I could tell she remembered what they'd done to her. She began blowing and clacking. I let her do it. I didn't like that she was afraid, but she looked kind of fierce when she did that, and I wanted the people from the market to be afraid of her.

The policemen led us up some steps and put us in a kind of wooden box, with rails all around, set up high in the middle of the room. They took off our chains, and then the two policemen stood behind us. Next to me, Papa was like ice, ice so cold that if I reached out and touched him, it would burn the skin off my fingers. My bear was on the other side of me, warm and dark. I put my arm across her shoulders and she got quiet.

At the front of the room, a man in black was sitting in a high leather chair behind a wooden box, writing. Who was he? He couldn't be the magistrate—he was just a little runt of a man. A magistrate had to be a very great man. This little man had to sit up high just to see over the box. With only the top of him showing, he looked like a puppet in a street show.

The Puppet stared hard at us. "Officer Pikche," he boomed, "what is that bear doing in my courtroom?"

Mustache answered him. "The bear is material evidence, Your Honor."

He must have been a magistrate after all. I guess we weren't important enough to get a big one.

"This is highly irregular, but let's proceed. What are the charges?"

"Theft, Your Honor."

"Have we evidence?"

"Yes, Your Honor." Mustache stepped down from the

box. At the police station, they'd taken everything out of my pockets, my whole morning's work. Now Mustache opened a little sack and laid everything out on a table— the crowns, the half crowns, the coppers, a ring, a bracelet, and a locket. A good day's work, but it seemed so very little, down there on the table.

I looked at Papa's face. Did he see what I'd gotten? The ring? The locket? Papa's lips moved, as if he was speaking to himself. I edged closer, but I couldn't hear his words.

Then the Puppet said, "Call in the witnesses."

One by one, the people from the market stood up. The men pulled off their hats and ducked their heads. The women smoothed their dresses. Then they walked up to the table and pointed to what they claimed I'd taken. Even the ones I hadn't taken anything from—the squirrel-eyed cobbler, the sooty-faced coal carter, and the woman who'd smelled of grease.

I leaped toward the railing. I wanted to shout at them, You're lying, I never took a thing from you. But then I looked at the Puppet and I thought maybe I'd better keep quiet.

When the last person had gone to the table, the Puppet stopped writing and looked up. "Just a minute. There seems to be a problem here. The amount that these people claim was stolen from them is many times the sum of the coins here on the table."

I could have told him they were lying. They not only gave us a runty magistrate, they gave us a stupid one.

"Since the truthfulness of these witnesses is in question, there will be some difficulty proving the charges."

"Well, Your Honor, there is one more witness, a very important witness."

"Call him in."

The gentleman in the fur-collared coat marched into the room. Everyone on the benches became quiet.

Papa whirled toward me, his eyes burning.

"Is that the man, Benno? The one with the gold watch who caught you?"

Papa grabbed my shoulders, about to shake me, but the policemen pulled him back.

"Yes, Papa," I said, and pressed closer to my bear.

"The accused will be silent," the Puppet roared at us. Then he turned to the gentleman.

"Forgive the interruption, sir. Please describe for us what happened."

The gentleman pointed to his soft leather purse and said that I had stolen it from him. He didn't shout, the way he had in the market. His voice sounded almost sleepy. One slow finger at a time, he took off his gloves, reached into his pocket, and brought out his watch.

"The little ruffian was trying to steal this, too, when I caught him."

He meant me, but he never looked at me.

The Puppet turned to me. "Boy, you've been accused of the attempted theft of this man's watch and the actual theft of all those items. What is your name?"

Everyone's eyes turned on me. Papa looked at me, too. Then he leaned over and hissed in my ear, "Tell them nothing, Benno. They will do what they want with us, but you will not help them do it."

"Boy, you will speak to me," said the Puppet. "I asked you your name."

Looking straight ahead, Papa said quietly, "Tell him your name."

"Benno."

"I can't hear you, boy, speak up."

"My name is Benno."

"Who taught you to be a thief?"

I wanted to shout out, I'm not just a clumsy thief. I don't hold a knife to people or sneak into their houses when they're asleep. I'm better than a thief. I take people's money while they're standing right next to me, and they never even know. My papa taught me, and he was even better than I am.

But I didn't say a word. I only looked at Papa and kept quiet.

"You'll look at me," the Puppet said, "when I speak to you, boy. I asked you who taught you to be a thief."

"Nobody, mister. Nobody taught me."

"Magistrate Hookim. You will address me as Magistrate Hookim."

It looked like he was staring at me, but he was wearing little, glittering glasses, and I couldn't see his eyes.

"Answer me, boy. Someone taught you to pick pockets. Was it your father?"

I couldn't say anything, so I put on my best face, my sweet-little-boy face. And I smiled like the sun.

"Why are you smiling like an imbecile, boy? Do you not understand the seriousness of your crime? I surmise that it was your father who taught you to pick pockets."

I wanted to rush out of that box, I wanted to run up to the Puppet and scream at him, Don't you know? It was me! I did it! Papa taught me to do the work, but it doesn't matter who taught me. I did this! Me! I'm the one! Papa never once got caught. I did!

Suddenly I realized that the rich gentleman—the one with the gold watch—was like Cousin Simor. When Papa got the better of him, Cousin Simor never forgave Papa. Then a terrible thing happened. Papa was sent away from his family, away from his village. I'd gotten the better of the gentleman. And now, because of that, something terrible was going to happen to us.

I could feel my bear watching me. I moved closer to her and, down low, so no one could see, I took her leg and held on to it.

Hookim looked at Papa. "Sir, the boy refuses to answer. Perhaps you will be more cooperative. Was it you who taught this boy to thieve?"

Papa stared straight at the Puppet, but he did not speak.

"Your silence, sir, will do you no service. I advise you to answer me. Did you teach this boy to be a thief?"

"The boy is not a thief," Papa growled.

The Puppet put both his fists on the table and leaned forward angrily. "Sir, if you lie to me, it will go all the worse for you. I give you one last chance to tell me the truth."

Now I could feel Papa growing angry. The Puppet couldn't see it. Papa's face showed nothing. The policemen couldn't see it. Papa never moved from his spot. But Papa was standing right next to me, and I felt it.

I held on tighter to my bear's leg. She turned her head to me and began licking my cheek.

The Puppet stared hard at Papa for a long time. Then he said, "Since you have nothing to say in your own defense, I must conclude that you have been an accomplice in this theft, possibly even the cause of it. For that crime you shall serve six months in the National Prison."

Now Papa's anger had grown so large that it burst out of him. He threw himself against the railing and raised his fists. "A thousand curses on your miserable head! May you burn and shrivel in hell! You and your fancy gentleman and all those pox-riddled people there." And he began to punch out with his big fists and kick the railing with his heavy boots.

I threw myself across my bear. She was trembling. Papa couldn't get at Hookim, but I was caught in the box with him. At any second I expected to feel his fists on me.

"Officers, restrain that man," Hookim screamed.

The two policemen grabbed Papa's arms—he was strong and they had to struggle to chain his big hands behind his back.

"It's all right now, Bear," I whispered.

As I said that, the second policeman began to drag Papa, still muttering curses, out of the box. I started after him, pulling on my bear's chain for her to come with me, but Mustache held me back.

"You stay here, son. You can't go with your papa now."

But we had to go with Papa to prison! My bear and me, we didn't have anyone else. And Papa had no one but us.

"One moment, Officer." Hookim was screeching now. "Sir, for your disorderly conduct in this courtroom, you shall serve an additional month in prison. Officer, you may remove the prisoner now."

The policeman tried to pull Papa away, but he stood strong, not moving. Then he looked down at me. All the anger had gone from his eyes. He looked as though he wanted to pull me against his chest, but his hands were chained. I tried to speak, but no sound came out.

The policeman tugged at Papa's chain, and he followed the policeman out of the box and out of the courtroom. The door shut behind him, and he was gone.

I sank to my knees and hugged my bear around her neck. I had to think, to figure out what we would do until Papa came back.

"Stand up, young man." It was Hookim.

Wasn't he done yet? Why couldn't he just be quiet and let me think? But I stood up.

"Young man, your behavior and your morals are disgraceful. You shall be remanded to the Public Residence for Wayward Youths."

I didn't understand. I knew that he was sending us somewhere, but where? I had never been anywhere without Papa. I began to sweat, and my ears rang. The market people were all laughing behind their hands.

"Silence!" Hookim's voice boomed.

"Excuse me, Your Honor." Mustache was speaking. "May I approach the bench, Your Honor?"

"If you must."

When Mustache came back, he was smiling. The market people, the policeman, all of them were smiling, laughing. Only my bear wasn't laughing at me. I scratched the top of her head.

"Benno."

It was Hookim again. I wished he would shut up.

"You will look at me, boy, when I speak to you."

Why should I look at him? He couldn't make me. Why didn't he just send us to that place, wherever it was, where I'd never have to see him again.

Mustache whispered in my ear, "You'd better do as the magistrate says or he may change his mind."

So I looked up. If I didn't do what he said, he might give me an extra month in prison, the way he'd done to Papa.

"Benno, you are a very fortunate boy. I have agreed to remand you to the custody of Officer Pikche here. That means that Officer Pikche will take charge of you. As for the bear, it shall spend the rest of its life in the Zoological Park, where it can harm no one."

What did he mean? Wasn't my bear going with me?

"No!" I screamed. "You can't take my bear away. I have to take care of her. She'll die without me."

But Hookim wasn't listening. He was sitting behind his box and writing. I had to make him understand about my bear.

"Please, you've got to listen to me—"

The Puppet looked up then, but not at me, at Mustache.

"One more thing, Officer Pikche. Please arrange for the boy to attend school. And report back to me if he presents any problem."

I was wrong to think that Old Hookim would understand. He was a magistrate. But Mustache . . . Last night he'd understood about me taking care of my bear. He'd let me stay with her and brought food for us. Holding my bear's collar, I stood in front of him. "Please let me keep my bear," I said to him. "I'm all she knows. She won't be any trouble, I promise. She doesn't eat much. I'll find food for her. And I'll clean up after her. She won't be any trouble at all."

"I'm sorry, son. It was up to the magistrate."

"But you talked to the magistrate before, and he listened to you. He'll listen to you now."

"Magistrate Hookim put you in my custody, but I'm positive he'd never give me custody of the bear." Mustache looked at my bear and patted her head. Then he looked at me and smiled. "Besides, your bear will be better off where he's sending her. Your bear'll be fine, I promise you. And so will you."

I hated him and his smiling face.

7

No Escape

M Y BEAR WAS PACING up and down, watching me. She wanted to go home, to her pen and her dinner. And that's where I was going to take her.

We'd been put in a little room, and we were supposed to wait there until Mustache came for me and the zookeeper came for my bear. But no one was going to take my bear. I picked up her chain and opened the door.

A policeman, broad as a barrel, was sleeping in a chair beside the door. As I slipped out, my bear moved close to me, and her chain clanked against the wooden floor. The Barrel jumped to his feet. My gut jumped, too, right up to my chest, but I tried not to let it show. I looked straight at the Barrel and smiled like the sun.

"The officer said we could leave whenever we were ready, so we'll be going now."

Holding my bear's chain with one hand and her collar with my other hand, I started down the hall.

"Hold on a minute!" The Barrel stepped in front of me. "My orders are to keep you in that room until someone comes for you. Now take your bear back in there and don't give me any trouble."

"That room's awfully small. My bear can hardly move in there. Couldn't I just walk her up and down in the hallway?"

I turned and started to lead her away, but he grabbed my shoulder.

"Try something like that, and I'll have to put shackles on you. Now get back in that room."

"All right. But I'm going to need a shovel pretty soon."

"A shovel? What for?"

"Well, my bear'll have to go pretty soon. I can't just leave her droppings on the floor. If you'll get me a shovel, I'll clean it up for you."

"Not my problem. The scrub woman'll worry about it. Now just take your bear and go back in that room."

"The scrub woman'll need a mop, too. All right, you don't have to push me."

The door clicked shut behind us. I waited, but I didn't hear a key turn in the lock. I put my eye to the keyhole. I could see right out into the hallway. If I turned my head to one side and squeezed against the door, I could even see the Barrel sitting in his chair. I knelt on the floor a long time, looking through the keyhole. My bear lay against my leg, and I stroked her head. Needles pricked my leg, but I didn't move. Then the Barrel's head fell back, and he started to snore.

I stumbled to my feet. My bear stood, too, and started after me.

"No, you've got to stay here, Bear," I whispered. "Stay and wait for me. And be quiet."

She knew those words. She rolled her eyes up at me, but she lay down and didn't make a sound.

I pulled off my boots and edged myself out the door. At one end of the hall there was a wall, but at the other end I could hear voices. I slid my bare feet along the smooth wooden floor until I came to a balcony. Down below was a big room, as noisy and crowded with people as the market in summer.

The market. A greenish sick feeling rolled up from my belly. I mustn't think about that now. I had to get us out of here. I could snake right through the crowd and get away. But my bear couldn't. Everybody would see her.

I hurried back. The Barrel was still sleeping. My bear was lying right where I had left her. Her eyes followed me, but she didn't move or make a sound. I dropped down beside her and pressed my head against her rough fur, feeling her warm breath on my cheek.

It was just like every morning, when we sat together in her pen, waiting for Papa. But Papa wasn't coming. *Six months in the National Prison . . . An additional month in prison.* Papa would be in prison for seven months. And me . . . *Officer Pikche will take charge of you.* Mustache was going to lock me in a cell somewhere, and I'd stay there until Papa came home. Papa would be coming home. And then I would, too. But my bear . . . My bear wouldn't ever come home. *The bear shall spend the rest of its natural life in the Zoological Park.*

She'd die there. I remembered when Pepi's mouse died. Mice don't live very long. But a bear lives a long time. Molmo forgot to feed his dog, and the dog ran away. But I never once forgot to feed my bear. She'd never run away from me.

A park. I'd seen the parks the rich people had, where babies were wheeled around in fancy little carts and boys rolled hoops and sailed little boats in the fountains.

A park would be a good place for her. She'd like living there. But she wouldn't like it if the boys laughed at her and poked her with their hoop sticks. Then she'd have to stand up tall and show them her teeth and her claws. They'd never bother her after that.

"Bear, listen to me." She sat up. "Bear, we can't run away together. But the magistrate said you're going to go to a park." She was looking into my eyes, trying to understand what I was saying. She didn't know the words I was using. "A park. There'll be flowers, grass. Maybe even a tree. The grass'll be soft to sleep on, even better than straw. And the tree'll keep the sun off you in the summer."

But now it was winter. The grass would be dead, under snow and ice. Would they put down straw for her?

Where would she go to get out of the cold and the rain? And who would feed her? Take care of her? I stroked her muzzle, and she licked my fingers. I'd always taken care of her, ever since she was a cub. Back then she thought I was her mama.

"Bear, maybe your mama will be there, in the park. Maybe that's where they send bears when they catch them. Your mama'll be happy to see you. And proud, too, you're so big now and so smart. You won't need me, Bear, you'll have your mama."

I hoped she believed me. I didn't know for sure that her mama would be in the park, but I wanted her to believe it. I wanted to believe it, too.

I heard a voice, and then the door opened. I jumped to my feet, and my bear stood up next to me. A man in a green uniform, the thinnest man I'd ever seen in my life, came in.

"Looks like this is the right room. I've come to take the bear."

"Don't come any closer. She's wild." I poked my bear in her ribs. That was her signal to stand up on her hind legs, showing her teeth and her claws. "You'd better back off! She can be vicious. She could take your hand off with one snap of her teeth."

The skinny man didn't even look at me. He was peering at my bear's face. "I'm a zookeeper. It's my job to take care of animals. I know a tame bear when I see one. Now just let me look her over and then we'll be going."

He came over to my bear, reached out his hand, and started feeling her back and her ribs, working his fingers through her fur. Then he moved up to her head. He tried to open her mouth, but she clamped it shut and backed away. The man didn't say anything. He just reached out and stroked her calmly, along the back of her neck, gentling her. When she quieted, he eased her jaws apart. I moved up next to her and held on tight to her neck.

"This place you're taking her, it's a park, isn't it?"

"A park? Well, it's called the Zoological Park."

"That's it, that's what Magistrate Hookim called it."

"We just call it the zoo."

"The zoo. But aren't there trees? And grass? A fountain?"

"Well, sure. All around the outside—trees, grass. No fountain, though."

"And animals? Is there a bear?"

"Sure, there'll be a bear."

I put my mouth to my bear's ear and whispered, "You see, it's just what I said. You'll be with another bear. Maybe your mama. Anyway, it'll be a nice place. This man won't hurt you. You can see that, can't you?"

My bear twisted her head around and licked my cheek. She understood.

The zookeeper picked up her chain.

"No, not yet. You can't take her yet." I tried to yank the chain from the zookeeper's hand, but he held it fast.

"It's getting late." He shrugged at a small barred window. "I want to be back at the zoo before dark."

The zookeeper tugged at her chain, but my bear stood like a tree rooted in the floor. He pulled harder, but still she wouldn't move. She wasn't going to go with him until I told her to. And what if I didn't tell her? Then we could stay here together. But I knew that would never happen. They'd come and drag me away, and then they'd take my bear.

"You go now, Bear. Go."

Still she wouldn't move. Then I raised my fists to her, as though I was about to hit her, and I shouted, "Go!"

I turned away from her and shut my eyes. I could hear her claws clicking on the floor, then the door shutting. Then nothing.

When you throw a piece of paper into the fire, first the edges flame up. Then they turn black, and the paper curls in on itself. After a bit the whole paper is gone. Nothing is left but a little pile of ash. I felt like that.

I heard steps outside. Were they bringing my bear back? I ran to open the door. Two policemen were walking away, leaving the hallway empty. I was about to shut the door again when I saw something stuck on the doorjamb—a patch of my bear's fur.

I took the fur in my hand and sat down on the floor, a little pile of ash holding a patch of fur.

8

Snow and Shadows

ALL AFTERNOON, I crouched in a corner of the room. The room smelled of my bear. Everywhere I looked I could see her.

I kept my eyes on the gray sky outside the small, high window. But snow was creeping up the glass. The room was growing darker.

When the window was nearly white, the door opened and Mustache came in. His helmet and the shoulders of his overcoat were hills of snow. He smelled of wet wool.

"It's time to go, son."

I stood up, shoved the patch of fur into my jacket pocket, and held out my hands for the chains. Mustache looked at my hands and gave me the gray blanket from my cell.

"You'd better wrap this around yourself. It's an evil night out there."

Outside, there was no moon. Black clouds hid the stars. The wind whipped hard, and icy snow splintered against my face and ears. I pulled the blanket up over my head and held it close around my neck. The street lamps were too weak for the storm. Their dim yellow light died halfway to the pavement, so I couldn't see where we were walking. All at once my feet slipped on the icy cobblestones, and my legs twisted out from under me. My arms flopped wildly. Mustache's hands caught me around my chest.

My blanket had fallen to the pavement. He picked it up and tried to wrap it around me.

"I can fix my own blanket!" I shouted, but the wind pulled my voice away.

He was acting like he was my papa. Well, he wasn't Papa. I wondered if Papa was out in the storm, walking to that place, the National Prison. They'd taken him hours ago. I hoped he was already there, inside.

But my bear was going to a park. I thought about all the parks I'd seen, trying to remember if any of them had a place where she could get out of the storm. I remembered one park that had a little round house where a band played in the summer. The house was open on the sides, but there was a wall in the back and a roof on top. I hoped the park my bear was in had a place like that. The wall would protect her from the wind, and the roof would keep the snow off. But she'd be huddled there, waiting for me to bring her supper.

Would the zookeeper remember to feed her? He was so skinny, maybe he didn't eat much himself. Would he give some of his food to her? He said it was his job to take care of the bear. He'd better do his job right.

The snow and the darkness made everything strange and quiet. Even the sound of our footsteps was swallowed up.

We rounded a corner into a narrow, unlit street. Here the houses nearly touched each other, shutting out the wind. Me and Papa, we were always back in our room by the time it got dark, and we never walked in streets like this one. I knew what was waiting for us here—cutthroats! They made you give them whatever you had, even your clothes, and if they didn't like what you gave them, they slit you from ear to ear.

Mustache must be in league with the cutthroats. He wasn't taking me to a cell. He was taking me to be killed! They'd led my bear away because they knew if she was with me, they couldn't get me. A cutthroat would take one look at her sharp teeth and long claws, and he'd pocket his knife and slink away.

Suddenly a shadow rose up in front of us. I tried to wrench free of Mustache, but his grip was too strong. He was holding me so the cutthroat could get me!

"It's all right, Benno." Mustache's voice sounded as if it was coming from far away. I saw him raise his nightstick high. "I don't think that thug will want to tangle with a policeman."

The shadow melted back into the darkness. I moved closer to Mustache as we pushed on. I felt his thick arm against my shoulder. For a moment it felt like walking next to Papa.

At the end of the street, there weren't any houses. A gust of wind blew me to one side, and I felt an iron railing pressing against my arm. I knew that railing. We were on the Middle Bridge. But tonight there were no carts or carriages, no drays or wagons. Once in a while we came upon other people, their heads bent against the wind, their hands clinging tight to the railing, fighting their way through the rising snow. Below the bridge, I could see nothing in the blackness except for a few boat lights tossing wildly.

If this was the Middle Bridge, was Mustache taking me back to the Stalls? Was Papa there, in our room? And the bear in her pen? When Mustache had talked to old Hookim, he'd made him change his mind about me. Maybe he'd made Hookim change his mind about Papa, too, and my bear. Maybe we were all going home.

"We're soon there—" The wind whipped the rest of his words away.

He must mean the Stalls.

"My bear, is she there already?"

"I can't hear you, son. Wait till—"

But at the end of the bridge, we didn't turn down toward the Lowlands District, toward the Stalls, we turned up, into the Middlebridge District. I wasn't going home,

I was going to a place I didn't even know. I felt like my head was going to burst. I'd been stupid again. If Mustache didn't want the cutthroats to get me, it was because he had another plan. I'd have to start being smart.

In the Middlebridge District, the houses were low and shuttered against the storm. But at the end of one street, yellow light spilled out of two windows and pooled onto the snow.

"There's our house, right up ahead. We'll be warm and dry in a wink."

Mustache loosened his hold on me, and I yanked my arm free.

"Come on, son. You've braved the storm this far. You can make it. I'll help you."

Something in my head said, Run, run now. The snow is thick, he won't be able to see more than a few feet ahead. You could get away from him.

And then what? I asked myself. I'd surely freeze to death in a street somewhere.

I remembered something else—Mustache catching me when I fell and wrapping my blanket around me. And his voice saying, "It's all right, Benno."

Whatever there was in that house up ahead had to be better than freezing to death. Or being killed by cutthroats. Unless. Unless in that house there was a den of cutthroats, and Mustache had brought me there so it would be easier for them to rob and kill me. No, I was being stupid again.

Mustache took my arm and began to drag me along, like the ironmonger pulling his mule. When we reached the lighted windows, I could see that they were wide and low, like shop windows. A bell jingled as Mustache opened the door. The sudden brightness made me shut my eyes.

I tried as hard as I could to open them—but the light was too strong. I smelled fresh bread, sweet and warm. Then I felt my hand being taken by a hand with soft skin and strong fingers.

"Hello, Benno. I'm Katorna Pikche."

It was a woman's voice. Cutthroats were never women. I squinted and saw that the woman was very tall and straight, with pink skin and shiny black hair and eyes. Behind her was a counter, and behind that a wall of shelves with baker's baskets on them. So this must be a bakery.

Mustache tried to put his arm across my back. I shrugged it off.

"Well, Kat," Mustache said, stamping the snow from his boots, "I've never been so glad to get home as I am tonight."

"I did my share of worrying, Pik. I won't even tell you what was going through my head." She took a deep breath. "Well, the two of you are here now, and we can all rest a lot easier."

Not me. I had a lot of things to think about.

9

Stoves and Stew

"BENNO, COME INTO THE KITCHEN, and we'll get some of those wet clothes off you. You must be frozen to the bone." The woman started toward a door in the back of the bakery.

"Pik," she called over her shoulder, "would you close the shutters, please? And put out the lamps, we won't be needing those now."

Behind me, the shutters rattled down. I was trapped. I'd been hoping to escape as soon as the sun came up. But if I tried to pull those shutters up, the rattling would wake them for sure.

I followed the woman, all the while looking for another door. My feet were so frozen I couldn't feel them. She led me into the biggest kitchen I'd ever been in. And the warmest. A big, brick baker's oven covered nearly one whole wall. Next to the oven was a narrow door. I saw a wider, green door on the opposite side of the room. Was one of those doors unlocked? Did one of them lead outside?

On the back wall was a big black cookstove. Me and Papa, we had a cookstove, too, a little one. Ours was rusty, and we'd put bricks under it where one leg had broken off. The door you put the coal into only had one hinge, and it dropped down crooked when you opened it. But this stove was shiny black with lots of bright silver hinges and handles. On top of the stove was an enormous pot. The smells coming from that pot made my belly knot up. If they didn't lock me in tonight, I was going to come back here and eat everything in that pot.

"Come over here, Benno." The woman was standing next to the oven. It was the oven that was making the kitchen so warm. Now my feet were coming unfrozen, and it felt like knives were stabbing them. The pain pushed everything else out of my head.

"We need to get that blanket off you. It's so full of ice it could almost stand up by itself." The woman reached for the blanket. I should have pulled away from her, but the hot room had made me slow.

The blanket crackled as she peeled it off. Then she reached toward my jacket.

"I can do that!" I wasn't going to let some woman take my clothes off, as if I was a little baby.

My fingers were so stiff I could hardly open my buttons. The woman stood in front of me, waiting. Why did she have to keep watching me like that?

She was hanging my jacket and the blanket on a line in front of the baker's oven when Mustache walked in. He sat down on a bench and patted it for me to sit beside him. He began taking off his boots and stockings. I was struggling to pull off my boots when the woman turned around.

"The boy's not wearing any stockings! Who would let a boy go out in such weather without any stockings!"

"Kat—" Mustache shook his head at the woman.

"I never wear stockings. I don't like them. They make my feet too hot."

The woman knelt down and touched my feet. "Your feet don't feel any too hot to me. They're like two blocks of ice." She started rubbing them with a rag. At first I didn't want her to do that, but as she rubbed, the pain began to go away.

"All right now, Benno, Pik'll take you to your room, and you can take off the rest of your things there."

This was it, now they were going to lock me up. I hated to leave that warm kitchen.

"This way, Benno." Mustache started toward the green door on the other side of the kitchen.

Behind the door was a staircase. I started down toward the cellar, because that was where the cells had been in the police station.

"Not that way, Benno. We're going up."

So my cell was upstairs. Well, up wouldn't be so bad, not as cold and damp as a cellar.

Mustache was a few steps above me, and my eyes were even with his feet. They were small and white and knobbly. I never thought about policeman having small, white feet. Mustache took me up two flights, to the top—just like our room at the Stalls.

He opened a narrow door and went in. I stayed behind on the landing. I saw a light go on in the room, and then he came back out again.

"This will be your room, Benno."

My room? I looked in. It was the whitest room I'd ever seen. There was a high bed, with sheets, a pillow, and a feather bed on top—all white. I stepped inside. Not a spot of grease on the walls, not a speck of dirt on the floor, not even a smudge of soot on the lamp. I went to the window and pulled back the ruffly white curtains. Outside, the snow had stopped. Under the window was a small table, with a water pitcher and a basin and a white towel hanging on the side. There was a round rug on the floor, all bright colors twisted together. But there wasn't any sleeping mat. I guessed I'd be sleeping on the floor.

"Who sleeps in the bed?"

"You do."

"Me? Who gets the floor?"

"No one, Benno. There'll be no one in this room but you. I think you'll find the bed nice and warm. The stove's cold, though." Mustache had his hands on a kind of tower in the corner, covered in white tiles. "I'll get some coal and start the fire."

"That's a stove? How am I supposed to put a pot on it?"

"A pot?" He laughed.

I didn't like his laughing at me.

"This isn't a cookstove, Benno. Kat does all the cooking down in the kitchen. This stove is just for keeping the room warm. You take off your clothes, and I'll be back in a minute."

Was he crazy? I wasn't going to take off all my clothes and stand there in my bare skin. I slid the window up and looked out. A slice of moon moved out from behind a cloud, and I could see a few stars. Below me was a sloping roof covered in snow. It was too dark to see all the way to the ground.

I shut the window and looked in the chest opposite the bed. The drawers were empty, except for white paper at the bottom of each one. I reached into my pocket, took out the patch of my bear's fur, and put it into the back corner of the top drawer.

Behind me, the door opened. I tried to quickly shut the drawer, but it stuck halfway. I was still trying to shove it closed when Mustache came in. I turned around, keeping my back against the chest. He had a bucket of coal in one hand and a long, striped shirt in the other.

"There's nothing in the chest, Benno. Mrs. Pikche's planning to buy you some new clothes tomorrow."

Mustache set down the bucket and wiggled the drawer back in. "That drawer sticks. I'll have to shave it down a bit."

I was glad he hadn't seen the fur.

He wasn't wearing his police uniform anymore. Without his helmet, he seemed about a foot shorter. He looked like he might be smiling at me. I couldn't tell for sure, because his mustache was so bushy, but I saw its ends rise.

"Here." He held out the shirt. "I brought you one of my flannel nightshirts to put on. Take off your wet clothes and we'll hang them on the line downstairs."

He pulled open a small door in the thing he called a stove, threw in the coal, and picked up a poker. I ducked behind the bed. But he just stoked the coals with the poker and stood it back up next to the stove.

"By the time you come up to bed tonight, this room'll be nice and warm. Well, go ahead, take off your wet things."

I pulled off my shirt and dropped it onto the floor.

"Don't do that! Kat doesn't like her floors getting wet and dirty." He came around the bed, stooped, and picked up my shirt. "Give the rest of your clothes to me."

I stood up and quickly pulled the nightshirt down over my head. Then I reached under it and slipped off my trousers. The nightshirt hung way down on the floor. The sleeves covered my hands.

"Roll up the sleeves, and I'll tie this cord around your waist. Then we'll just pull the nightshirt up over the cord and you'll be fine."

"This is a dress! I look like a girl in a dress!" I would have ripped it off, but Mustache was holding my clothes.

"It's not a dress. You have to wear something to sleep in."

"Me and Papa, we sleep in our underdrawers."

Once I said it, I knew I shouldn't have told him that. At least I didn't tell him that in summer, me and Papa didn't sleep in anything. "My underdrawers are warmer than this nightshirt. At least they are when they're dry."

Mustache laughed. "Well, things'll be a little different for you here. You'll get used to the new ways, Benno. Now wash your hands and face and then come down to supper."

First a bed, then a nightshirt, now washing. This wasn't how I thought it was going to be. But it was a lot better than the cell. And he did say supper. I washed fast.

As soon as I opened the kitchen door, I could smell it— the sweet, juicy smell of meat and onions and potatoes, all cooking together. Whatever they gave me for supper, I was going to make sure I got some of that stew. The woman was standing at the stove, dipping a spoon into the pot. She brought it up all brown and dripping, put it in her mouth, and smacked her lips. I could taste the stew just from the smell of it. She put down the spoon and looked me over.

If she laughs at me, I'm going to run right out of here, I thought. Even though I couldn't run anywhere—barefoot and looking like a girl.

"You look a lot less frozen than when you first walked in. I've set a cup of tea on the table. That should warm your insides."

The long table was as white as a peeled potato and just as smooth. Different from Papa's and mine. Ours was small and brown and rough. The cups were different, too—thin and white—they weren't tin that burned your lips. I wrapped my hands around the cup, and the warm, sweet tea steam floated up at me. I smelled honey in it.

As the woman began slicing a loaf of bread, I heard a scratching noise outside the room. She opened the door next to the oven. I couldn't see where she'd gone, but I heard her footsteps on a brick floor, then a bolt being slid. I decided that must have been an outside door, because a gust of wind blew across the kitchen. So when I needed to, I could get out that way.

The woman walked in holding a cat against her chest and scratching its cheek. This cat was fat, not like the ones in the alleys. Its brown, striped fur was so thick it nearly swallowed up her fingers.

"Benno, this is Pum. Pum, meet Benno. Benno's going to be staying with us for a while."

I was sure that the cat didn't care who I was. He didn't even look at me, just rubbed his mouth against the woman's face. She set him down, and his big paws thumped on the brick floor. Then she took two tin plates and spooned some of the thick brown stew out onto one plate, poured milk from a pitcher into the other, and set them down in front of the cat.

Stew! For a cat! I could have eaten that stew. And my bear would have liked it, too, and blinked her eyes and licked her paws after she ate it.

The cat rubbed against the woman's legs. Then he sniffed the stew and walked away. Just walked away—as though the bowl was empty! Well, that was all right. I'd come and get it later.

"Too hot for you, Pum? Well, let it cool and then you'll eat it. Pum's been with us for years, Benno. I got him to keep the mice out of my flour bins, but he's more than a mouser now. He's become a good friend. Pik, we'll need another chair at the table."

There were already three chairs at the table. A chair at the end, a chair on the stove side, and a chair opposite that one. Why did they need another one? Mustache put a fourth chair on the side away from the stove.

"Come on, Benno. Let's sit down."

He pointed me to the chair across from the stove. The woman was spooning the stew out onto three plates. Three plates. That cat wasn't the only one who'd be eating stew! She put the plates on the table and sat down. The plates were like the cup, thin and white, with little blue flowers.

I stabbed a chunk of meat with my knife and started to bite into it.

"Benno, why don't you use your fork?"

I put the chunk of meat back on the plate, pushed it off the knife with my fork, and lifted it toward my mouth.

"No, Benno. Put the meat on your plate, hold it there with your fork, and cut a small piece with your knife. Then you can eat it."

By now, I was so hungry for that stew I had to swallow hard just to keep from drooling. I was pretty good with a knife—not as good as Papa, but pretty good. And a fork was easy, you just stuck it into the meat. But I couldn't work both of them at the same time. First the meat slipped out from under the knife. Then, when I finally got the meat cut, it fell off my fork.

It looked like I wasn't going to get anything to eat after all. Maybe that was their plan, to put good food in front of me and not let me have any of it. Just when I was getting ready to pick up the plate and dump the stew right into my mouth, it all worked—the knife, the fork, the holding and the cutting. I bit into a chunk of the softest, best-tasting meat I'd ever had in my life.

That woman was really something. Didn't like her floors getting wet, made it hard to eat. But she was a good cook, and she did keep filling my plate with more stew and passing me more bread so I could mop up the gravy. Me and Papa always bought day-old baker's bread, when it was hard and dry. The bread we gave the bear was what the baker threw away. Only her teeth could bite through it. But this bread was white and soft and sweet.

I needed to save some of the bread for my bear, but the nightshirt didn't have any pockets. I'd have to come down for it later.

"Benno, Pum's finished his supper. Watch what he does now."

The cat had licked his bowl clean. He walked slowly toward the empty chair next to me, sat back on his haunches, and, like a spool of thread unwinding, jumped onto the chair. Then, so quickly I hardly saw him move, he hooked a slice of bread, dropped it onto the chair seat, and began nibbling it.

"Pum can't resist Mrs. Pikche's bread." The corners of the man's mustache were rising again. "We used to try to stop him, but he's too smart for us. So we just let him take his slice of bread, and then he's happy."

That cat was just like a baby, a dumb, fat baby. Well, let him have his baby bread. As long as he didn't take it off my plate.

"Ready for some cake, Benno?"

The woman took away the plates and brought over a cake with red jam on top and nuts around the sides. She cut a slice, put it on a plate, and handed it to me.

I'd never had cake before. I'd seen cakes in shop windows, but I'd never eaten one.

"Let me know how you like this, Benno. It's my best recipe."

How was I supposed to eat the cake? The woman had a knife, the one she cut the cake with, but she'd taken away my knife with my plate. I wished I had claws, like the cat, so I could hook the cake the way he hooked the bread.

"Don't you like cake, Benno? You're not eating any."

"You took away my knife."

Mustache smiled. "That's all right. The cake's soft enough that you can eat it with just a fork."

I ate the white, crumbly cake first, then the crunchy nuts, and saved the sweet, slippery jelly for last. The rest of the cake was sitting there, on a plate in front of the woman. I couldn't stop looking at it. She cut me another piece. My belly began to ache, not because I was hungry, but because I'd eaten so much. I'd had even more to eat tonight than when Papa made mushroom stew. And those nights we didn't have cake.

The cat held one paw in front of his face, spread out his toes, and carefully licked each one. I guess he didn't want to waste any either. Then he licked the inside of his front leg and wiped it across his face. When he was done, he jumped off the chair, curled up by the bake oven, and went to sleep.

Mustache pushed his chair back from the table. "Thank you, Kat, that was a delicious meal." He patted his stomach.

Then he looked at me. "Benno?"

What did he want?

"Benno, shouldn't you say something to Mrs. Pikche?"

"You want me to say something?"

"I think you should say thank you."

Maybe I should. It really was the best supper I'd ever had in my life. Or probably ever would have again.

"Thank you. The food was really good." I smiled at her—not my smile from the marketplace—a real smile.

"You're welcome, Benno."

On the wall near the stove was a big sink. The woman poured in some hot water from a kettle and started to wash up the dishes. The man dried them and put them away on shelves.

While their backs were to me, I got up from the table and walked around. Beside the door to the bakery was a shelf. And on the shelf stood an iron money box, just like the ones the merchants put their money into. It had a clasp on the front where a padlock would fit, but there wasn't any lock. I lifted the lid, taking care not to make a sound, and slipped my fingers inside. Three small bins. Very slowly, so that the coins wouldn't clink, I dipped my fingers into each bin. One had crowns, the second half crowns, and the third coppers. Altogether, there was more money in that box than me and Papa ever got in a month.

"Benno." It was the woman. "Leave the money box alone. It doesn't belong to you." She still had her back to me. If that woman's fingers were as good as her ears, I could have taught her the work.

Mustache turned to face me. He wasn't smiling. "Stealing is a crime. I don't want to have to do it, Benno, but if you steal while you're under this roof, I'll have to turn you over to Magistrate Hookim. Do you understand?"

I didn't smile either. I just stared back at him.

"Pik, Benno needs some time. Benno, it's late, so you head up to bed now. We'll see you in the morning."

Upstairs, my room was as warm as the kitchen. I put out the lamp and crawled under the feather bed. It was light and soft. Papa would never believe I spent the night in a bed like that. I began to feel as if I was falling into a snowbank.

Suddenly my body jerked awake. I'd heard about snowbanks. I'd heard that people fell into huge drifts, and even though they were freezing to death, they didn't feel it, they got fooled and thought they were really warm. Were the policeman and his wife trying to fool me? Would everything be different in the morning?

I lay in the bed for a long time, waiting. Then I crept back down the stairs. I couldn't hear any sound from the kitchen, and I didn't see any light under the door. I was just closing it behind me, when something sharp bit into my leg.

I jumped and crashed into the table.

Had they heard? I waited, afraid even to breathe. But no one came down, and the door stayed closed. It must have been that stupid cat. I wanted to kick him, but I was afraid he'd squawk.

The brick floor was rough under my feet. On one side of the kitchen was the money box. On the other side was the bread box. I decided not to take the money until I was ready to leave. In the meantime, I'd take the bread for my bear.

Back in my room, I put the loaf in the drawer, next to her fur.

10

Out with the Old

THE ROOM WAS TOO WARM, and the bed was too soft. I kept waking up. And every time I woke up, I thought I was in my own room with Papa. My head kept saying, No, you're in the white room at the Pikches', but my eyes saw our table, our rusty stove, saw Papa in his bed. I knew I wasn't dreaming—my eyes were open.

The sun struck my face. I slid out from under the feather bed and stepped onto the chilly floor. Where the sun struck the windowpanes, the frost was melting. I pressed my forehead against the icy panes and looked out. Melting snow dripped from the roof above. Below me, in a little fenced-in yard, the snow sparkled, but I could see it was melting also. Too far below for me to get out that way. Besides, I didn't need to climb out the window. They hadn't locked me in my room last night. I could leave if I wanted to.

My bear was in her park—outside. I hoped the zoo-keeper had put her in a place with a roof over it. And he'd better have given her food. If I could bring her here, she'd have plenty of food. And I could keep her in that fenced-in yard.

It would be almost like before, at the Stalls, with Papa and me upstairs and my bear down below in her pen. Except I wasn't in the Stalls, and Papa was in prison. And they'd never let me bring my bear to their yard. I'd asked Mustache, at the courthouse, to let me keep my bear. I'd told him I'd find food for her, clean up after her. But he'd said no, and acted like I should be happy they were taking my bear away. Well, I'd better stop dreaming.

I couldn't run away in a nightshirt. I went downstairs and found my dry clothes folded on the bench in the kitchen. And there was food on the table—little currant buns and a pot of jam. The cat was gone. If he'd been there, he would have hooked every one of those buns and eaten them all. I jumped into my clothes. I was about to stuff the buns into my pockets when the woman came in from the bakeshop.

"Well, good morning, Benno. You slept late this morning. The kettle's on, and the tea leaves are in a tin on the shelf, next to the cups. I see you've found your clothes."

"They were dry, so I put them on." Did she think I was going to wear that nightshirt all day and walk around looking like a girl?

"Well, wear your old clothes this morning, but this afternoon—my goodness, it's nearly afternoon already—this afternoon we'll go and get you your new clothes."

I knew the old-clothes man's place was in the Lowlands District, not far from the Stalls. He lived in a basement and kept his wares in bins. It was dark in the basement, and after Papa'd scrabbled through the bins and found a piece of clothing, he'd take it out to the street to look at it in the light, checking for thin spots and holes. Then they'd haggle, and when Papa got a price he liked, he'd pay it, but he'd grumble that the old-clothes man was a thief, and the old-clothes man would whine that Papa was taking bread out of the mouths of his babies.

When the woman had gone back into the bakeshop, I ate some of the buns and put the rest in the drawer with the loaf of bread. Then I sat down by the window and tried to plan what to do. If I stayed here awhile longer, I could save more food for my bear. Then, when I did run away, I'd have plenty of bread for her. Maybe I could talk the woman into letting me keep my old clothes instead of selling them. Then I could sell them. We'd need the money. Besides, in another day or two the snow would all be melted and I could get around the city easier to look for my bear. Yes, the best thing was to stay here for a while.

That afternoon, the woman closed up the shop. I watched her as she took some money out of the money box and put it into her purse. I could tell she hadn't taken all of it. So there would be some for later.

Outside, the snow was melting fast in the street, but someone had swept the sidewalks dry. I turned down toward the Lowlands District.

"Not that way, Benno. We're going to the barbershop first, to get your hair cut."

Papa always cut my hair—when the weather got warm in the spring, and at the end of summer. I didn't like the idea of someone else touching my hair.

The barber was smacking a razor against a leather strap when we walked in. The top of his head was as bald as a peeled onion. A bald barber! I wanted to laugh, but I didn't, because he was holding the razor and the strap.

"The young man would like to have his hair cut, please."

No, I wouldn't, I wouldn't like it at all. I wanted to turn around and walk right out of there.

Onion-Head pushed me down onto a chair and pulled off my cap. I yanked it away from him. He squeezed his fingers roughly through my hair. "That is a rat's nest! It looks as if it hasn't been cut in months."

The woman smiled at him. "But you give such excellent haircuts. I'm sure you'll make Benno look quite handsome."

She was good, she was really good. Just as I thought, if her hands were as good as her mouth, she'd be made for the work.

"You know that I'll have to charge you extra for this haircut. It'll be a lot more difficult to do."

"Well, when we bring Benno back for his next haircut, I'm sure you'll find it much easier."

Onion-Head took a comb out of his pocket and yanked it through my hair. From another pocket, he took out a scissors and started cutting at the back of my head, where I couldn't see what he was doing. But I did see thick piles of hair lying on the floor like brown caterpillars. By the time he'd finished, there was a hill of caterpillars. Maybe he wanted me to be as bald as he was. I felt the top of my head. He'd left me some hair, but not much.

Onion-Head picked up a bottle of some sweet-smelling stuff.

"No tonic today, thank you. Benno will wash his hair when we get home."

"Well, considering what I had to start with, I think I gave him a rather nice haircut. Here"—Onion-Head handed me a mirror—"have a look for yourself."

I hardly knew the boy I was looking at. Papa always cut my hair a little ragged. He said I mustn't look like a little rich boy. But this time my hair wasn't ragged at all. I went to touch my hair, but stopped—I didn't want to mess it.

The woman opened her purse and counted out some coppers. Not too many. There would still be a lot left.

"Benno, let's go and get you your new clothes."

We were still walking in the wrong direction, but I thought maybe she went to a different old-clothes man.

"Here we are," she said.

Instead of taking me down to a basement, she went into a shop. The store was wide and bright, and the two sidewalls had cabinets all the way up to the ceiling, with glass doors and all sorts of clothes in them. In the back, there were more clothes hanging on rods. This wasn't like any of the shops near the Stalls. The merchant came skittering out from the back, a little man, with waxy hair, like the head of a beetle, and tiny feet.

"Good afternoon, gracious lady. How may I help you this afternoon?" The Beetle smiled, a stiff smile, as if it was painted on a doll's face, and kept his eyes on the woman.

"We'd like some clothes for the young man, if you please."

The Beetle looked at me and stopped smiling. He squeezed his mouth into a little ball.

"If Madam will permit me to say so, I don't believe my emporium would have anything suitable for this ragamuffin. Perhaps another shop—"

That was fine with me. I started toward the door. But the woman reached out and marched me back. Standing very straight, she tipped her chin up and looked down at the man's beetle head.

"We should like a jacket and trousers, long ones, not breeches, for school. Also, everyday trousers, several shirts, stockings, underdrawers, two nightshirts, boots, and a cap. An overcoat and a muffler. And, oh yes, a half-dozen pocket handkerchiefs."

The Beetle skittered away. The woman's eyes were laughing.

After a while the Beetle came back carrying a stack of clothes taller than he was and laid them on a counter.

The woman worked her way down the pile, picking up a jacket or a pair of trousers or a shirt and looking at it carefully. Just like Papa used to do. But what was she looking for? These clothes were new, there weren't any thin spots or holes in them.

"What do you think of this jacket, Benno, do you like it?"

Did I like it? I didn't understand what she was asking me.

"Here, try it on, Benno. Let's see how it fits."

The jacket was blue, thick and warm with shiny buttons. The old-clothes man wouldn't ever get this jacket.

"Well, Benno, the jacket fits you well. Do you like it?"

"Oh, yes, I like this jacket."

The Beetle was practically dancing, trying to please the woman. When we'd picked out everything, he wrote up the bill, and the woman checked it over. I moved closer to her and looked at the bill while she was checking it. All these clothes were costing too much money, money that I was going to need later.

"You don't have to buy these clothes. I already have a cap. And I don't need a muffler. Or pocket handkerchiefs."

"Don't be silly, Benno. Winter's not over yet—you'll need all these things. Even the pocket handkerchiefs."

All right, then, I'd get more for the clothes when I sold them.

At the house, the woman opened the door next to the bake oven. I looked in and saw a storeroom lined with shelves of food and big bins. On the back wall, there was a door to the outside. A great tub stood in the middle of the floor.

"I'll get your bath ready for you, Benno."

"My bath! In the winter? I'll catch my death."

Me and Papa didn't take a bath in the winter. In winter, our room was cold, and if we took off our clothes and stood with our feet in the little washtub, we would have nearly frozen. And the towel was so thin, by the time it was my turn to use it, it was soaking wet, so I just got right into my clothes. We never took a bath until the weather warmed up.

"You'll take a bath, Benno. And you won't catch cold. The oven keeps this room warm enough."

"I washed my hands and face last night. Before supper."

The woman wasn't even listening to me. She just kept pouring water into the tub. Then she poured in several kettlefuls of boiling water.

"Now, the soap's here and the brush. When you're undressed, leave your old clothes outside the door."

Why was she still standing there? Was she going to wait while I got undressed?

"I can wash myself."

"Of course you can, Benno. Wash your hair, too, and behind your ears, your neck, your back. And make sure to do a good job on those fingernails. When you're done, there are towels on the rack, and I'll put your new clothes here on this chair."

A bath. In the winter. She really did want to kill me.

I didn't want to take my clothes off. Suppose she walked in on me. I opened the door a crack and looked into the kitchen. The woman was gone. I took off my clothes, pushed them outside the door, and shut it again quickly. I put one foot into the water. It felt good, so I climbed in. The tub was so big I could lie back in it. I'd never done that before. I was almost falling asleep when the woman called through the closed door.

"Don't forget the back of your neck, Benno. And your ears. And use the brush."

She was back, and there wasn't any falling asleep now. If I didn't get out of that tub in a hurry, she just might decide to walk in on me. I washed fast, climbed out and pulled a towel around me, watching the door the whole time.

The towel covered nearly all of me. I rubbed myself dry and put on the new clothes. There were no holes in anything, not even the stockings. The underdrawers weren't scratchy. The shirt had all its buttons. And the trousers came all the way down to my feet. They'd be fine on a cold day in the market. Best of all were the boots. Brown and smooth, they gleamed just like the rich men's purses. I didn't want to put them on right away. I held them to my face and rubbed my cheek against them. They smelled better than chestnuts.

But there was another smell coming from the kitchen, a smell like burning garbage. I threw open the door. The woman was holding my clothes, about to toss them into the fire.

"Wait! You can't throw my old clothes away. I might want to wear them."

"Don't be silly, Benno. I've already burned your old boots. The soles were worn right through. And these clothes are more holes than cloth. Besides, they smell something awful."

"Well, there's something in my pocket I need." I grabbed my old breeches and pulled out the little silver knife. I had to keep my old cap, too—I might need it.

"And I want my cap."

"I can't see why, but all right, you may keep the cap, Benno. And Benno, speaking of keeping things . . ." Her voice got quiet. "While you were bathing, I went up to your room to put away the rest of your new clothes. I found the loaf of bread and the buns in the drawer. Benno, you don't need to hoard food here. There's always plenty. You won't go hungry."

I rushed up to my room and yanked open the drawer. The patch of fur was gone. I tumbled down the stairs and into the kitchen.

"Where is it? What did you do with it?"

"With what? What did I do with what?"

"The fur, the fur that was in the drawer with the bread."

"You mean that clump of hair? I didn't want that filthy thing next to all your nice, clean clothes. I shudder to think where that piece of hair might have come from. Something you picked up off the street—"

"I didn't pick it up off the street. It was my bear's fur. It wasn't filthy. Where is it? I want it back."

The woman's eyes turned cloudy.

"Give me my fur. I want it back." I pawed wildly through my old clothes, trying to find the fur.

"Oh, Benno, I burned it."

"You burned it? You burned my bear's fur?"

All the warmth from the bath ran out of me. I started to shake.

"I didn't know, Benno. I'm sorry. If I had known . . ."

She reached out her hand, but I jumped away from her. I wanted to tear off all my new clothes and throw them at her, but my old clothes were gone, burned up, and I couldn't go looking for my bear in just my skin.

11
A Witch and an Oven

ALL THROUGH SUPPER, whenever I looked at the woman, I saw her in front of the fire, burning my bear's fur and the food I'd saved for her. She didn't care about my bear. All she cared about was having everything clean—me, my clothes, everything in her whole house.

But I also heard her saying, "I'm sorry, Benno." I knew how sorry felt. I was sorry for a lot of things.

Supper was thick slices of meat, with sweet cabbage and the good bread. The last thing was an apple cake. I wanted to eat it, but the apples were brown. I kept thinking of the rotten apple I'd eaten once when I'd been so hungry I couldn't stop myself. I poked my fork into the cake and pushed the apples to one side.

"What's the matter, Benno?" Mustache asked me. "Don't you like apples?"

"I like apples."

"Then why—?"

"I ate a rotten apple once and it made me sick."

"Benno. What makes you think these apples are rotten?" The woman's face seemed a little angry.

"They're brown and they're soft. That means they're rotten."

She smiled. "The apples are brown because I sprinkled them with cinnamon powder. That's a spice. And they get soft when they're baked. Eat the apples, Benno. You won't get sick."

After supper, the woman said, "I think I'll read a story this evening."

So we pulled the chairs over to the bake oven—they kept a slow fire there all night—and Mustache took out his tools and started fixing a chair leg, and the woman took down a black book with gold letters on the front and started to read. The cat jumped into her lap, closed his eyes, and curled his tail over his face.

The story was about a boy named Hansel and a girl named Gretel. It started off all right, but pretty soon I was worrying. Because the story told about a witch. A witch with a cat. The witch seemed all sweet and kind at first, but that was only so she could catch little boys and fatten them up with all sorts of good food. And then, when they were nice and fat, she threw them into her oven and roasted them so she could eat them.

Maybe the woman was going to fatten me up and eat me. Right then I decided to stop eating. I wished I hadn't eaten so much supper.

That night, in bed, I kept remembering the story. Was that woman a witch? Maybe those apples really were rotten, after all. But I didn't have a bellyache. After a while I started to think about my bear and Papa. Then my belly did ache. But I knew it wasn't from the apples.

Early the next morning I got dressed and crept down the stairs. I was going to look around. Maybe there were bones from the other boys. But the woman was already in the kitchen.

"Well, good morning, Benno. I'm glad to see you up early this morning. You can help me with my baking."

I guess she thought I was fat enough already. I would have run, but the doors were still locked. I had to keep my guard. If the woman tried to grab me and throw me into the oven, I'd have to grab her first and throw her in. Just like Gretel did.

The witch made me wash my hands, even though I'd had a bath yesterday. She set out a big yellow bowl and put a brown powder into it. Was that brown powder poison? Or was it that same stuff she put on the apples? I'd eaten that and it hadn't hurt me.

She poured some water from the kettle into a cup and said, "Check this water, Benno. It should be warm, but not hot."

I was about to drink the water, when she said, "Don't drink the water, Benno. Put a drop on your wrist. If the water feels not too hot and not too cold, then it's just right for the yeast."

She had me pour the water into the bowl, add some sugar, and then stir it.

"A little sweetness and a little warmth and the yeast will come alive."

Alive? Could the witch make boys out of yeast and water?

"Watch it, Benno, and see what happens."

I was watching all right. Out of the end of my eye, I could see the witch take a bigger bowl and do the same thing with the yeast and the water and the sugar.

The brown stuff in the yellow bowl was starting to bubble.

"Good," she said, "the yeast is alive. Now I'll scoop some flour into the bowl and you stir it."

The more flour she added, the harder it got to stir. Maybe she wanted me to get so tired from stirring I'd fall asleep, and then she'd throw me into the oven. She had her sleeves rolled up, and I could see that she had very strong arms. If she grabbed me, I might not be able to break free.

Just when I thought I couldn't pull the spoon one more time, she said, "Your dough seems about ready. Take a handful of flour and rub it over the table."

The flour felt cool and soft, like a lady's velvet sleeve I once touched. She scooped the dough out of the bowl onto the table.

"Now," she said, "we'll knead the dough."

Maybe she needed the dough. I needed to make sure she didn't bake me in the oven.

"You knead it like this, Benno." She took the dough from her bowl and pushed her hands into it. Then she pulled the dough over itself, turned it, and pushed it again. "Do the same with your dough, Benno. Push it away from you and pull it back."

The dough felt good under my hands, squishy and warm. I pushed and pulled, pushed and pulled for a long time. After a while the dough started to move, like my bear's skin when I combed her fur. Maybe it was alive. Maybe there really was a boy in there! A witch could do that—put a boy in the dough. I looked hard, but I couldn't see anyone.

"That dough seems to be ready for its first rising. Here, put it into this clean bowl and cover it with the towel. Now put it on this shelf, by the oven where it's warm. That's fine. We need to leave the dough alone for a while, let it grow."

Let it grow? Into what, a boy?

"I'm going to start some more breads, but you keep checking this one. When it's twice as big as it is now, you tell me."

I did watch. For a long time, nothing happened. Then it grew, but not into a boy, just into a bigger lump of dough. I told the woman.

She pushed two fingers into it and said, "Now turn the dough out onto the table again, punch it down, and knead it a little bit more."

We did the whole thing all over again. The dough got bigger—but it was still just a lump of dough. This time she patted the dough into two round balls and put them onto pans. Then she turned to the oven and opened the door.

I jumped back, ready to run.

"Hot, isn't it, Benno. You'll get used to the heat when you've done a lot of baking."

Or if I was the one being baked, I thought.

But the only things she put into the oven were the pans of bread. And the only things that came out were hot, brown loaves. I guessed I didn't have to stop eating after all. Which was good, because when the baking was done, the woman put some bread and buns on the table. Then Mustache came down, dressed in his policeman's uniform, and the three of us sat down to eat breakfast.

"I think Benno's going to be a big help to me here, Pik. He has the makings of a good baker. Where's Pum? Wouldn't he like to try Benno's bread?"

"I let him out just a little while ago."

I was glad of that. I hadn't made the bread for that dumb cat to eat. I was going to take it to my bear.

When we'd finished, the woman said, "I'm going into the shop now, Benno, and Pik's going on patrol. You look like you could use some fresh air. Why don't you go to the backyard? No, better not. It's quite muddy back there. Go out front and stay on the sidewalk. If you get hungry, take some bread and cheese. Take some apples, too. But don't go far. And be sure to come in before dark."

As soon as they had both gone, I stuffed the bread and cheese and a couple of apples into my pockets and headed out to find my bear. I went through the storeroom and out the back door so the woman wouldn't see the lumps in my pockets.

I felt all watery inside, starting out. I knew every inch of the Lowlands, and the zoo park wasn't there. I thought I'd better start in the Middlebridge District. I was looking for a park. A park with trees. The trouble was, there were trees all over the Middlebridge District. Some streets had trees down both sides. I'd see all those trees, and my chest would jump. But it was never a park, just a line of trees.

At the end of one street, I turned the corner and nearly walked right into a group of gentlemen. I pulled off my cap and ducked, thinking they were going to thrash me with their sticks, but they just looked me over and went back to talking.

I realized it was the fine clothes. The gentlemen thought I was a proper boy! I tried walking right down the middle of the sidewalk, as bold as I could be. I walked right by ladies and gentlemen, and the ladies never pulled their skirts away and the gentlemen never raised their sticks. Some of the ladies even smiled at me.

My chest was jumping. I was a proper boy now, and I could walk all over the city, anywhere I pleased! No one would chase me or curse me or take a stick to me! I could walk across the street to that toy store, stand and look in the window and think which toys I'd like to have. I'd like that big toy boat, the one with a man with a long white beard standing on it and animals walking right up the gangplank. I'd like to have that boat and the animals, too. There were animals I'd never seen and didn't know the names of. But I knew two of them—the bears.

The watery feeling came back. I wasn't a proper boy. I was still Benno, and I needed to find the park where they were keeping my bear. On one street, I did find a park, a little one, with trees and bushes and benches to sit on. But I could see right away there weren't any animals. It was just a park, not the zoo park.

I walked the whole length of every street, down to the river and back up. I walked every street on this side of the river. But I didn't find my bear. It was getting dark and cold. The watery feeling inside me was turning to ice.

I headed back to the bakery. I went into the kitchen through the back door and up to my room. I hid the bread and cheese under the mattress, where the woman wouldn't find them.

12

A Toad, a Grub, and a Snort

I'D BEEN STAYING WITH THEM FOR A WEEK. We were all at supper. I had my fork in one hand and my knife in the other, ready to cut into a thick cabbage loaf stuffed with meat. My mouth was watering.

Then Mustache said, "I stopped in at the school today, Benno. You're to start on Monday."

My mouth went dry.

"School . . . This whole time I've been here, I didn't go to school. Why do I have to go now?"

"We thought you needed a few days to get used to things, Benno. But all children from the age of seven to fifteen must be enrolled in school. It's the law."

The law! Me and Papa never worried about the law—except to stay away from it.

"But I've been helping you, haven't I? I carry in the sacks of flour and the firewood." I turned to the woman.

"And what about the baking? You need me to scrub the bowls and bread pans, sweep the floor, carry the trays of bread into the shop. I'm even getting to be a pretty good bread baker, you said so yourself."

"You've been a great help, Benno, to me and to Officer Pikche. And you can still help us, before you go to school in the morning. Now go ahead and eat your supper."

"I'm not hungry! You can just give my supper to the cat!"

"Benno!"

"Apologize to Mrs. Pikche."

"For what? I said I'm not hungry. And that cat will eat anything."

The woman's face was getting all pink. Mustache stood up.

"Benno, go to your room and stay there until you're ready to apologize."

I jumped to my feet, making my chair clatter to the brick floor, and then I stomped up the stairs. I was going to stay in my room past Monday. I was going to stay in my room until Papa came home and I'd never have to go to school.

But the next morning, the smell of baking bread came creeping up the stairs.

"It's a fine day, today, Benno. Sunny, dry—feels like spring is coming early this year."

Maybe it was a fine day for Mustache. Walking to the school, I felt as if I was slogging through mud up to my ankles. With every step I had to pull myself along. It wasn't any better inside the school. It looked as if the mud had washed through the place and left everything brown—the floors, the benches along the sides of the halls, even halfway up the walls.

"Mistress Dreiwatter used to be my teacher, Benno. When I was in her class, I thought she lived in the school. I might have been right. Anyway, just remember to do what she says. She's pretty strict. Here we are. This is her classroom."

Mustache knocked on the door. From inside, a voice like pebbles said, "Enter."

"Go ahead, go on in, Benno. And good luck to you."

The doorknob felt like mud, too. It slipped under my fingers.

The pebbly voice came again. "I said, Enter."

I pulled the door open a crack and squeezed myself around it. I couldn't look anywhere but down at the floor. I heard laughing.

"Silence, children. Resume your work."

When I raised my eyes toward the voice, I saw that it was coming from the oldest woman I'd ever seen. Her face looked like the riverbank in a dry summer, when the mud gets hard and cracked. Her hair was white and thin, so her skin showed, but wound around the top of her head was a thick yellow braid. The Old Crack-Face was sitting behind a high desk with books on it, and she was holding a long stick.

"Come here, young man."

I walked over and stood in front of her desk. She looked me all over, starting at my hair and going down to my boots. She had eyes so pale they were almost white.

"Your appearance is not what I had been led to expect. I presume you are Benno."

I nodded my head.

"You will answer, boy, when I speak to you."

"Sure, I'm Benno."

"You shall say, 'Yes, Mistress Dreiwatter.'" Her fingers were curling around the stick.

I didn't say anything.

She raised her stick.

"Yes, Mistress Dreiwatter."

"I have spoken with Officer Pikche about you. He has informed me of the circumstances under which you were put in his charge. I made it quite clear to him that I do not believe a boy of your sort belongs here. I am a teacher of children, not a warden of the criminal classes. The proper place for you is in the Public Residence for Wayward Youths."

She stopped speaking. The room had gone quiet. I felt as if I was underdrawers hung out on a wash line for everyone to see. Old Crack-Face put the stick down and pulled a lacy white handkerchief out of the end of her sleeve. She flicked the handkerchief across the tip of her long nose, the way a horse uses its tail to flick away flies. Then she tucked the handkerchief back into her sleeve and picked up the stick again.

"Nonetheless, Officer Pikche believes that you are capable of learning. That remains to be seen. Officer Pikche was not the cleverest boy in his class, but he was diligent and obedient. You would do well to follow him. Do you understand?"

I didn't understand half the words she said, but her fingers were still curled around that stick, so I said, "Yes, Mistress Dreiwatter."

She got up from behind her desk and walked over to the wall. A black slate was hanging there.

"Come here, Benno. Stand beside me. Look up, above the blackboard." She rapped her stick against a long row of numbers and letter. "These are the numbers from one to ten and the letters from *A* to *Z*. We shall begin with the numbers. Repeat after me. One."

"One."

She pointed to the next number. "Two."

"Two. I know all the numbers. They're easy . . . Mistress Dreiwatter."

"We shall see. As I point to each number, tell me what it is."

She began skipping her stick back and forth along the row of numbers.

"Five, three, seven, eight, four, five. I said that one already. Don't you remember?"

"I'll have none of your insolence, boy. Put your hand on the desk."

I put my hand out and she rapped the stick across it.

She wasn't strong, like Papa, but the stick was thin and sharp and cut into the knuckles of my hand. My eyes stung, but I didn't blink.

"How does it happen that you know your numbers? I was told that you have never been to school." Her mouth made a tight little knot.

"Papa taught me."

She lifted her stick again.

". . . Mistress Dreiwatter."

"I see. And did your father, the schoolmaster, also teach you your sums?"

"I don't know." I looked down at my boots.

"Look at me, boy, when I speak to you!"

I looked up. She had raised her stick again.

"You don't know if your father taught you your sums?"

"I don't know what 'sums' are, Mistress Dreiwatter."

Her mouth twisted into a nasty smile. "Sums are adding two numbers together, such as four and seven."

"Four and seven make eleven, Mistress Dreiwatter."

"Nine and six?"

"Fifteen, Mistress Dreiwatter."

"Is it possible that you also know how to subtract? Eighteen less five—"

"Thirteen, Mistress Dreiwatter."

"How is it that you know your sums?"

I wasn't going to tell her about counting up the money every day. Or about not letting the peddlers cheat us out of our change. "My papa's not a schoolmaster, but he's smart. He taught me lots of things, Mistress Dreiwatter."

"Well then, let us see what else he taught you. Recite for me the letters of the alphabet."

I felt hot all over. "I don't know them, Mistress Dreiwatter."

"You don't know the letters of the alphabet?"

"No, Mistress Dreiwatter."

Behind me, I heard laughing.

"Silence, class." She picked up her stick and pointed. "This is the letter *A*. Repeat after me, Benno. *A*."

"*A*." I'd seen all those letters before. But I didn't know their names.

"*B*."

"*B*."

As she went on saying the names of all the letters, it wasn't her voice I was hearing. It was Pepi and Mohno, when they first started school. They'd sit outside and read from a book they called their first primer. There was a letter on each page and a picture. The pictures told a funny story about a boy and an apple tart. I liked the pictures, but I thought Pepi and Mohno were showing off about reading the letters. Now I wished I'd learned them.

Old Crack-Face made me say all the letters over and over, after her. Then she told me to say them by myself, but I couldn't remember all of them. Everyone was watching me. I could feel their eyes on my back, and I could hear them laughing. They thought I was stupid.

I wasn't stupid. I just didn't see the point of all those

letters having names. Letters weren't real. When I looked in my cap, I could see four coins—four was real. Or seven. And seven was better than four. But what good was a *Q*? Or a *T*?

All those kids laughing at me thought they were so smart. But they wouldn't be so smart if they tried to do the work. I'd be the one laughing at them. They couldn't ever learn the work. And I couldn't ever learn those letters. *Learn the letters, stupid. Learn them so she'll let you go and everyone won't think you're stupid.*

Then I had an idea. I was good at remembering people. *Think of those letters as people,* I told myself. *Make each one a person.* So I made each letter a different person or thing. An *R* was a fat lady taking a walk. A *K* was a soldier marching. And I started to remember them.

"You must also learn to write the letters, Benno. This is your copybook, and here is a pencil. Follow me."

As I turned around, I saw the other kids. They weren't my age. Most of them were younger than me. They'd put me in a class with little kids. Did they put me with the little kids because I was small or because I couldn't read? But I could do my numbers.

"Benno, this will be your place."

From the front of the room to the back, there were long lines of slanting tables, with two kids at each one. The boys were on one side of the room, the girls on the other. Old Crack-Face was standing next to a table with only one boy sitting at it.

The table was right in the front of the room. She'd be able to see everything I did.

"You shall sit here, next to Erdweiss." She pushed down a little flat seat that was hinged to the table in back of it. "The boys behind you are Petrolin and Bogwald.

"Open your copybook to the first page, Benno. Begin with the number one. Copy it neatly across the entire line. When you have done with the number one, copy the number two across the next line. When you have completed the numbers to ten, take a fresh page and copy the letters, beginning with the letter *A*."

She walked back to her high desk and began writing something.

I felt Erdweiss staring at me. When I looked over at him, I thought I should have been the one staring at him. His skin was white, like a fish, and his face had scabs all over it. He kept picking at them.

"The first thing you got to learn, if you want to live to your next birthday, is to call us by the names I tell you. I'm Grub." He was whispering so Old Crack-Face wouldn't hear him.

"Him, he's Toad." He pointed at the kid behind him, the one named Bogwald. Toad had a fat chin, and his mouth hung open like a trapdoor. Every once in a while he snapped it shut, like he'd caught a fly.

"And he's Snort." He pointed to the other kid, Petrolin. He had yellow hair. I'd seen stuck-up kids like him. They thought everyone was always looking at them. So I didn't.

These three weren't as young as the other kids in the class. But I knew they'd never be my friends. I could feel them laughing at me.

"Toad and Grub and Snort. You got that?"

"Sure. I'm Benno."

"Well, we're going to call you Dummo. Too dumb even to know the letters."

Grub kicked me in the leg. I kicked him back, harder. He tried to kick me again, but I swung my legs out from under the table, and he kept missing me. He must have gotten tired of missing, because he put his copybook on his lap and lifted the tabletop to put the book inside. My copybook and pencil went flying off the table and splattered onto the floor.

I grabbed the edge of the table lid and slammed it down on Grub's fingers. He let out such a yelp that Old Crack-Face hurried over, her stick in her hand.

"Erdweiss, why are you creating a disturbance?"

Grub was sucking on his fingers and couldn't speak. But Snort, behind him, said, "It was Benno, Mistress Dreiwatter. He smashed the lid of the desk on Erdweiss's fingers." Snort had a high up-in-his-nose sort of voice.

"We shall see whose fingers are smashed." She rapped her stick across my knuckles, but I didn't let my fingers even twitch. "Now, Petrolin, if there is any further misbehavior from Benno, be sure to let me know."

"Oh, I shall, Mistress. I certainly shall."

I shall, Mistress, I certainly shall. Petrolin wouldn't ever get smacked.

The three of them seemed pretty happy with themselves. Toad and Snort were jabbing each other with their elbows and poking their fingers in Grub's back. They'd better be happy now. I'd get them back, and then they'd be sorry.

I tried to take hold of my pencil to copy the number one. But my knuckles still hurt, and I had to switch the pencil to my left hand. My right hand was my clever hand, the one I always used for the work. My left hand wasn't so sharp. I pushed down too hard and the point of the pencil made a hole in the paper and broke. I had to take out my knife and whittle a new point and then brush the pencil shavings into the inkwell in the top of my table. The next time I tried not to push so hard on the pencil, but I still couldn't get it right. I wanted to make a straight line, but it kept running crooked. I tried over and over. After a while my hand and arm were aching so bad I couldn't even hold the pencil.

Then Old Crack-Face rang a little bell, and everyone stood up, formed a line, and walked out the door. I followed them. Was school over already? The line of kids went out a door at the back of the school, to a yard with high brick walls all around.

As soon as we were in the yard, a yell went up. The boys started running. I ran with them. The brick walls shut out the wind, and the sun shone straight down on us. I looked up at the blue sky. It was summer and I was running down the street, my bear beside me. I was fast, faster than anyone in the Stalls, and my bear was even faster than I was. Somebody thumped me on the shoulder and called out, "You're it." I pulled up short. A boy with round glasses was dancing around me, hopping from one foot to the other. My bear was gone. It was winter, and I was in a school yard. The boy with glasses ran off, but I was still faster than anyone. I caught another boy in a second and then he was it. The pack of boys ran after him, and I stopped to catch my breath.

Snort wasn't running with the rest of us. He was standing in the shadow of a wall, leaning against it. And Toad and Grub weren't running either. They were standing with a group of girls, arguing with one of them. Then Grub pushed the smallest girl to the ground. She started to cry and gave him something. The other girls gathered around the one Grub had pushed, but Grub and Toad walked over to Snort and handed him what they'd gotten. Snort looked at it, put it in his pocket, and they all laughed.

I couldn't believe what fools they were. Toad and Grub would walk right up to a girl—it was always a girl, never a boy—and make her give them something. If she wouldn't give it to them, they pushed her, or squeezed her arm, or kicked her until she gave it to them. Then they handed what they'd gotten to Snort.

The three of them were as clumsy as coal wagons. It was going to be too easy to get back at them. I slid up behind Snort, slipped my fingers into his pocket, and plucked out all the things Grub and Toad had given him. It wasn't anything much—a pencil, a spinning top, a few coppers. Then I stepped in front of him and put one hand in my pocket.

"Hey, Snort, lose something?"

Snort whipped his head around, looking for Grub and Toad.

"Looking for this?" I pulled a copper out of my pocket and held it in front of his face.

Snort's face got all red. I felt like Papa with Cousin Simor. Papa would laugh when I told him.

Someone called out, "Hey, Benno. Aren't you in the game?"

The boys ran over to see what was going on. On the other side of the yard, the girls were watching, too.

"How about this?" I held up the pencil. Toad's mouth dropped open.

"Or this?" The top. Grub scratched his scabs.

"Want these?" The rest of the coppers.

I walked over to one of the girls, with the boys following me, and gave her back her top.

I was giving back the pencil when Old Crack-Face blew into the courtyard like a windstorm. The boys opened a path for her straight to me. She grabbed me by the shoulder and screeched, "What have you stolen now, you filthy cur? Open your hands and let me see what you have there."

When she saw the coppers in my hand, her face went purple. "You little thief! Out with you! Out of this school and never come back!" She pointed with a stiff arm toward the gate to the street.

The yard was as quiet as midnight. Then one girl, a little, skinny girl, pushed her way through the ring of boys. "Benno wasn't the thief, Mistress. It was Toad and Grub and Snort." She spoke in a very small voice. "They stole the things."

She looked down at the ground, and her voice got so quiet I could hardly hear her.

"Benno was giving them back to us, Mistress."

"And who, may I ask, are Toad and Grub and Snort? Surely not pupils in this school?"

"Beg pardon, Mistress, I meant Bogwald, Erdweiss, and Petrolin."

"It is I who must beg your pardon, miss. I thought I heard you say that it was not Benno, but Bogwald and Erdweiss and Petrolin who have stolen this money."

"Yes, Mistress."

"Well, that cannot be. I happened to glance out of the window, and I saw this young hooligan . . . ! All I shall say for now is that nothing of this sort ever happened in my class before today. I trust that you will all"—and here she looked around at everyone but me—"that you will all guard your possessions carefully from now on." She looked hard at me.

"Benno, I am not a stupid woman. You may have deceived others in the past, but you will never deceive me. I shall be watching you.

"Children, recess is over. Return to the classroom."

WHEN MUSTACHE CAME HOME that night, I was waiting for him.

"You told her!"

"Told who? What?"

"Old Dreiwatter. You told her about me!"

"I had to, Benno. She asked how old you were, and I said I thought you were about eleven. 'Eleven?' she said. 'And only now starting school?' I said it wasn't your fault, that your papa had kept you out of school. 'For what purpose?' she asked. And then I had to tell her. I couldn't lie. But I told her you were a good boy, smart and hardworking and . . ."

I felt hot, and I could hardly breathe. My throat got tight and my eyes started to sting. I ran up to my room before Mustache could see me crying. Right then I decided never to go back to that school again. What difference did it make if I worked hard or I was good or smart. They didn't care. Only Papa did.

And my bear. She cared for me.

I reached under the mattress and felt for the bread. Every few days, I'd been taking out the stale bread and putting in fresh. I was going to need that bread tomorrow, when I found my bear.

13

Across the Bridge

IN THE STREET, other kids were walking to the school, but I was walking away from it, over the Middle Bridge. The day was fine, the sun was shining. I had on my school clothes, my new boots, and my old cap. Mrs. P. had made me a lunch—thick slabs of yellow cheese on her good bread, with a couple of apples and some sugar cookies. She thought I was headed to school, but I was going to find my bear.

The first park I came to was a small one with a fountain in the middle of it, but the zookeeper had said there wasn't a fountain at the zoo. The next park had an iron fence all around it. I was starting to climb the fence when a man passing by called out, "That's a private park, son. Only for residents."

"Isn't this the zoo?"

"The zoo? No, the zoo is over the bridge."

Well, he certainly didn't know anything. I'd come from over the bridge, and I knew the zoo wasn't there.

I'd walked most of the morning and hadn't found the zoo when I stopped to ask a shopkeeper in a white apron, who was sweeping her sidewalk.

"Over the bridge," she said. "Just over the bridge is where it is, in a big park."

Well, she didn't know anything either. Of course the zoo was in a big park. I knew that, but I also knew the park wasn't over the bridge.

Me and Papa, we'd worked all over the middle of the city. We walked miles to our work in the morning, and miles back home at night. But the walking had never seemed so long as it did that day.

It was well past noon. The sun was sinking lower in the sky, and I felt a heaviness sinking in my chest. Fine clothes or no fine clothes, I didn't want to be out after dark. But I had to find the zoo.

I asked a street sweeper.

"The zoo? Didn't know there was one."

I started walking away.

He called after me, "In a park, you say? Well, there's a park two blocks over. Maybe the zoo is there."

I'd just come from that park, and there wasn't any zoo.

A hansom cab was waiting at the curb. Maybe a cabman would know. He traveled all over the city.

"I think the zoo closes in the winter. Yes, I'm sure of it, the zoo shuts down in the winter. Won't open until spring."

Shut down! But then what had they done with my bear? Had they locked her inside? Would she be all alone until they opened the zoo in the spring? Or had they turned her out? Was she wandering the city now, looking for me?

I started to run, wild and frightened. I ran until a sharp pain stabbed my chest and I doubled over.

"What's the matter, boy? Are you hurt?" An old gentleman with a gray beard was bending over me.

I could hardly speak.

"I'm all right," I said, straightening up. "I've got to go, mister. I've got to find the zoo."

"The zoo, is it? Like animals, do you?"

"Yes, sir. But in the winter, when they shut down the zoo, where do the animals go? Do you know?"

"Go? Why, the animals don't go anywhere. They don't shut down the zoo. Shorter hours, I believe, but they don't shut it down."

"Please, mister. Can you tell me how to get there? To the zoo?"

"Well, I'm afraid you've gotten turned around. You're facing south, but the zoo is to the west of the city. Getting there's a bit complicated. Let me write out the directions for you."

The old man took out a notebook and a silver pencil and wrote something down. Then he handed me the piece of paper.

"Thanks, mister."

"But I wouldn't recommend you go today. It'll be dark by the time you get there, and they'll be closed. You'd best go home now and go to the zoo another day."

I stared at the piece of paper. There were the letters I'd been copying in school, and that's all they were—letters. The letters made words, but I couldn't read them. I folded the piece of paper very carefully and put it into my pocket.

I headed back toward the bridge. A skinny, spotted dog started to follow me. His eyes were brown, like my bear's, and they looked hungry. I knelt down and patted his head. He sniffed my hand, and I gave him my sandwich. As I walked away, I could hear him snorting and smacking his jaws.

IT WAS DARK when I walked into the kitchen. Mustache and the woman were sitting at the table, not drinking tea, not eating supper, just sitting at the bare table.

"Sit down, Benno." Mustache's voice was stiff.

"Two hours ago we had a visit from Mistress Dreiwatter. She told us you weren't in school today. Where were you?"

My knees went weak. I sunk into a chair and took off my cap. I hadn't thought about anything all day but finding my bear. I hadn't been thinking about what I'd tell them.

I did know one thing—I wasn't going to tell them I went looking for my bear. They only had a cat. They'd never understand about my bear. Besides, Missus P. thought my bear's fur was dirty.

They were both looking at me—waiting for me to say something.

"You aren't going to believe what happened to me. I almost don't believe it myself. This morning, when I was getting ready to go to school, I must have picked up the wrong cap by mistake, not my new cap, my old one. And—I know this is hard to believe—that old cap must have been enchanted, you know, like in the stories you read at night, Missus. It must have been enchanted, because the minute I put that cap on my head, my feet started to move all by themselves, and I couldn't stop them. They took me far away, to the other side of the city. I walked and walked—I was afraid I was going to walk my boots off, like those princesses in the story—but then, luckily, I got to feeling really warm, and I took my cap off to wipe my forehead.

"When I took off my cap, the spell was broken. I saw that I wasn't at school, but I didn't know where I was. I was lost. I was trying to find my way back when right in front of me, blocking my way, was a giant dog. He was as high as a church tower, and he had teeth like swords, and his eyes were burning like the sun. And he growled at me, with his big-sword teeth showing, and I thought I heard him say:

'Aroof, aroof, arroy,
I smell the blood of a boy.'

"I said, 'You don't want to eat me, I'm all skin and bones. If you let me go, I'll give you something better.'

"'A pile of gold?'

"'Better than that.'

"'A palace of diamonds?'

"'Better than that.'

"'Your kingdom and the princess's hand in marriage?'

"'No, even better. Something to eat.'

"And I gave the giant dog my lunch."

The woman was biting her lips, sort of frowning, but her chest was shaking with laughter.

"While he was eating, I ran away, but I heard him saying,

*'Aroof, aroof, arood,
This bread is very good.'*

"And that's what happened. But I won't make that mistake again—no more enchanted caps or giant dogs for me."

Mustache's hands were flat on the table, and he was looking down at them, not at me.

"Benno," he said, and he looked up. He wasn't laughing at all. "This is one of the hardest decisions I've ever had to make, but I must. You do recall Magistrate Hookim's instructions."

I remembered, all right. He'd sent my bear to the zoo. And he was going to send me to that place for Wailing Youths. Were they going to send me there now? I'd be locked away, the way I was locked in that cell. Only this time I'd be locked up without my bear.

"Magistrate Hookim said, 'Please arrange for the boy to attend school. And report back to me if he presents any problem.' Well, Benno, I did arrange for you to attend school, but you didn't go today, and now you have presented a very large problem. I have no choice but to report this to Magistrate Hookim."

"Please, Officer P., I'll go to school tomorrow. I promise. Please, Missus P., tell him. Tell him not to report me to the magistrate. He'll send me away. I don't want to go there, to that place for Wailing Youths. Tomorrow—I'll go tomorrow."

"Benno, go to your room now. Officer Pikche and I need to talk."

"Please, Missus. If they send me to that place, I'll never—"

"You'll never what, Benno?"

I remembered that first morning, when I'd looked out the window and thought that maybe I could keep my bear in the fenced-in yard. I knew better now. This place wasn't the Stalls. and that yard wasn't my bear's pen. I could never bring my bear here. She was my bear, not theirs.

I closed the door behind me and stomped up the stairs as though I was going to my room. Then I crept back down and listened at the door. The woman's voice was too soft to hear everything.

"Pik, you can't . . . Benno is right. You know the magistrate will . . . Pik, you don't want . . . any more than I do."

"Of course I don't, Kat. But I'm a police officer, sworn to uphold the law. It's my duty to report this." Mustache's voice was louder.

"Pik, listen to me. You've never broken the law in your life . . . the most honorable man . . . But Benno . . . Public Residence for Wayward Youths . . . respect for the law . . . know better, Pik. You know what he'll learn there . . . worse . . . keep him here . . . what Magistrate Hookim wants? . . . what we want?"

Mustache's voice got low for a long time. Then I heard him say, "I'll need to explain his absence from school. What reason can I give? I can't lie."

". . . Benno didn't go to school today, but he learned his lesson. . . ."

14

The Golden Bear

AFTER SUPPER THAT NIGHT, Missus P. got out the big black storybook to read from, the way she'd been doing every night. The other nights, Pum had circled around her, waiting for her to sit down, and then he'd jumped up in her lap and gone to sleep. But this night Pum circled around me, looking up at me with round yellow eyes. When I sat down, he put his front paws on my knees and sprang into my lap.

The woman looked up, her hands on the open book.

"A cat can be a good friend, Benno, when you need one."

I touched Pum's head. His fur was soft. He pressed his head against my hand, closed his eyes, and started making a chuffing noise in his throat and pushing his fat paws into my chest. Just like my bear when she was a cub. My chest and throat got tight, and I could hardly breathe.

"Hear him purr, Benno? That's where he got his name. He sounds like he's saying 'pummmmm.'"

My bear would be chuffing if I was with her. I tried not to think about her.

Missus P. began to read. "There was once a poor widow who lived alone in her hut with her two children, who were called Snow-White and Rose-Red, because they were like the flowers which bloomed on two rose-bushes which grew before the cottage. These two children were as good, happy, industrious, and amiable as any in the world. . . ."

This was not going to be a good story, I could tell. The girls' names were bad enough, but even worse, Missus P. was reading about how they went around picking flowers to put on their mother's bed. And every day they went into the forest to play—they didn't have to work or go to school or anything—and nothing bad ever happened to them.

I kept on petting Pum, and I wasn't really listening. Then I heard Missus P. say, ". . . a great bear poked his head in."

"A bear? Is this a story about a bear?" I asked.

"Yes, it is, Benno."

Now the story was a whole different thing. A bear was knocking at the door. He was freezing cold and he wanted to come in and warm up. They put the bear next to the fire, and Snow-White and Rose-Red brushed the snow off his fur. Missus P. was about to turn the page, but I stopped her.

"Could you show me where it says 'bear'?"

"Pull your chair over next to me, Benno, and I'll show you."

I scooped up Pum in one arm, picked up my chair, and sat back down again. Pum never stopped chuffing.

Missus P. pointed to the word "bear," and I looked at it. I knew all those letters—there was a *B,* and then an *E,* and an *A,* and an *R.* I ran my finger under the letters and said them.

"This word here—" I pointed to another word. "The letters are the same. What does it say?"

"It says 'bear,' Benno, just the same as before."

"You mean those letters always say 'bear,' all the time."

"Yes."

"And this word here is 'bear,' and this one, and this one?"

"That's right, Benno. I'll run my finger under the words as I read them, and you follow along."

She read about how the girls played with the bear and rolled all over him. But one time they thought it was funny to hit him with a stick. Well, then the bear shouted at them, "Children, children, leave me an inch of my life."

The bear stayed with them all that night, and after that, he came back every night and slept by the fire. When spring came, the bear told them that he had to leave and wouldn't be back for the whole summer. He said he had to go to the forest and guard his treasures from evil dwarfs. In winter, the dwarfs stayed in their holes under the ground, because they couldn't break through the frozen earth. But when spring came, and the ground was soft, the dwarfs broke out of their holes and tried to steal the bear's treasures.

The girls were really sad that the bear was leaving them. Snow-White could hardly open the door to let him out. The bear had to squeeze through, and a piece of his fur caught on the door. But Snow-White didn't feel the way I had felt at the courthouse. When she looked at the place where the fur used to be, she saw a glimmer of gold shining out.

The next time the girls went to the forest to play, they saw one of the dwarfs the bear had told them about. The dwarf's beard was stuck in a tree, and he was jumping all around like a dog with fleas. When the girls came by, he asked them to set him free. And those girls—they were really stupid—they did set the dwarf free. The dwarf knew the girls were stupid—he called them names like "foolish goose" and "crackbrained sheep's head" and "silly milk-faced creatures."

Those were good names for the girls, but they were even better names for Toad and Grub and Snort. I said them to myself so I'd remember them.

The second time those girls met the dwarf, his beard was stuck in a fishing line, and they cut him loose again. This time the dwarf called them "donkeys." The third time they met the dwarf in the forest, he was emptying a bag of shining jewels onto the ground. And those stupid girls stopped to admire the pretty colors. They didn't remember a thing the bear told them about his treasure. This was the bear's treasure—the dwarf had stolen it—and the girls didn't even try to get it back.

Just then the bear came walking through the forest. I could see him, rolling his big, shaggy head from side to side, thumping his big paws down on the ground. And when the bear saw the dwarf, he'd rear up on his hind legs, and his teeth and claws would gleam white and sharp.

When the bear came at him, the dwarf began to run, but the bear was too fast for him. The dwarf begged the bear to let him go.

"Spare me, my dear Lord Bear!" Lord Bear, I liked that. "I will give you all my treasures. See these beautiful precious stones which lie here? Only give me my life. What have you to fear from a little weak fellow like me? You would not even feel me with your big teeth."

But, I thought, the dwarf would surely feel the bear's teeth.

"Here, take the two wicked girls! They will make nice morsels for you! They're as fat as young quails! For heaven's sake, eat them!"

"Yes, eat them! Eat them, bear!"

"Did you say something, Benno?"

"No, nothing. Go on, keep reading."

The bear didn't eat the girls. Instead, he gave the dwarf

one swat with his paw and knocked him dead. And then the bear's fur fell away, and he was a man, all dressed in gold. He said that he was the son of a king. When the dwarf stole all his treasures, he had to wander the forest in the form of a bear until the dwarf was dead. Now that he had killed the dwarf, he had returned to his true self.

The rest of the story was all about the prince marrying Snow-White and his brother marrying Rose-Red. My bear would never marry a stupid girl like Snow-White. The end of the story was as bad as the first part. But I didn't care about that.

"Missus P., could you show me some more words?"

"Here, this word is 'Rose' and this word is 'Red.' They both begin with R."

"There's an R in 'bear.'"

"That's right, Benno. And here is the word 'Snow.' And here is 'White.' Can you find all those words in the story?"

And I did. Over and over again. Then I said, "Missus, could you teach me one more word?"

"Which word would you like to learn?"

"Can you show me my name?"

She walked over to a drawer and took out a pad of paper and a pencil. Then she sat down again and she wrote: *Benno*.

"That starts just the same as 'bear.'"

"That's right, Benno, the two words start just the same, but they end differently."

I took the paper and pencil from Missus P., and I wrote the word *Bear*. Next to it I wrote my name, *Benno*. And then, all the way down the page, I wrote the two words over and over again.

Then Missus P. put her hands on my cheeks. I didn't pull away.

That night, lying in my bed, I told myself the story, but only the good parts. I told about the bear with the gold shining through his fur. I took away the girls and put myself in. In my story, the dwarf was a puppet, all dressed in black, with little glittering eyes. When the bear swatted the dwarf, he set him to dancing so wildly that his little glittering eyes went spinning in his head. And after the bear dug up his treasure, he stayed a bear, and the bear and me went back to the house, and we were so rich that we were never hungry or cold again.

I told myself the story over and over again. And then I added one last part. When winter came, me and the bear were sitting by the fire in our warm house when there was a knock at the door. I opened it, and Toad and Grub and Snort were standing outside, half-frozen and shivering in the snow.

"Can we come in and get warm?"

"Get out of here, you crackbrained sheep's heads, you silly milk-faced creatures!"

"Please, Lord Bear, please, Lord Benno," they begged. "Do not turn us away. Let us in and we will give you all our treasures."

"Your treasures?" I laughed. "What are a few coppers to us? We have gold and jewels."

And I turned them out into the icy night and slammed the door shut.

15

"A Terrible Beast"

"GOOD MORNING, BENNO. How good of you to return to us."

"Officer Pikche sent a note."

"Well, I can be certain of one thing. You didn't write this note yourself."

Old Crack-Face bent over the note and then looked up at me.

"Officer Pikche writes that although you were absent from school yesterday, you have learned your lesson. Have you learned it, Benno?"

"Oh, I have, Mistress. I certainly have." I hoped I sounded like Snort.

"Well, we shall see. Take your place, please."

I had come back to school so I could learn to read. But all morning, all I did was sums.

"Two times two is four. Two times three is six. Two

times four is eight. . . ." Over and over we said the same numbers, until they all ran together in my head. Outside the window, the wind was blowing the clouds across the tin-gray sky. One of the clouds looked just like a bear covered with snow, like the bear in the story looked when he came to the girls' house. Those girls are hitting the bear with a stick. And now they're hitting me! Hitting me across my knuckles!

"Benno!" Old Crack-Face was standing in front of me, lifting her stick to hit me again. Her bony hand was shaking. She could hit me as hard as she was able to, I'd never cry.

"Benno, if you cannot keep your mind on your work, you shall have to sit in the donkey chair. Now recite for me, beginning with two times two."

I didn't have to recite anything. I could walk right out the door, out of the school, and never come back. Old Hookim could make me go to that place for wailing youths, but he couldn't make me go to school. But if I left the school, I'd never learn to read. So I recited the sums. All morning I recited them.

In the afternoon, Old Crack-Face called me up to her desk. Was she going to smack me again? I hadn't done anything bad since the last time she smacked me. I could have, but I hadn't. But Crack-Face's stick was lying across her desk, and she didn't even look at me. She was looking through a pile of books on her desk. She found the book she wanted and looked up at me.

"Benno, this is the first primer. Despite your abominable tendency to daydream, you have mastered the alphabet. I should like you to begin learning to read. Niera, would you come up here, please."

A very small girl stood up from her desk and walked to the front of the room. It was the scrawny girl from the school yard the first day, the one who stood up to Old Crack-Face and told her I hadn't stolen the coppers.

"Niera, Benno has never been taught to read. You will instruct him in the first primer, beginning with the letter *B*."

Old Crack-Face held out a small, dirty-looking book, and the girl reached out her hand for it. Her fingers were no thicker than splinters. She made me think of Pepi's mouse. It was a nice mouse, even if it did die.

The scrawny girl led me to the back of the room, looking down at the floor the whole time. We sat down together on a small bench—she hardly took up any space at all.

Opening the book to the first page, she put her finger under the first line and said, "The primer starts with the *B* sounds."

"Sounds? Isn't there a story?"

"That comes later. First you have to learn all the sounds. Then you put them together to make words. *Ba, be, bi, bo, bu*. As I point to each line, you say it, Benno?" She had a funny way of talking, very quiet, and she sounded like she was asking me a question.

"Say them, Benno. *Ba, be, bi, bo, bu?*"

"*Be,* that's like the beginning of the word 'bear.'"

"Mistress said you didn't know how to read."

"Well, she was wrong. I can read lots of words. I can read my name, and 'bear,' and 'rose,' and 'snow,' and 'white,' and 'red.' And lots more. When I want to."

"Can you read this?"

She turned to the last page in the book. I put my head close to the page and looked at all the words. There weren't any of the words I knew.

"I can read lots of words. But not these words."

"Benno!" It was Old Crack-Face, from her desk at the front of the room. "I don't hear you reciting."

"You'd better recite, Benno. Mistress will hit you again."

"I don't care if she does."

"If she hits you again, you'll have to sit on the donkey stool. And then you won't be learning anything."

The rest of the class was reciting, all together, their voices going up and down and up and down, like a saw cutting back and forth through a piece of wood. I wasn't listening to what they were saying, I was repeating *ba, be, bi, bo, bu, ca, ce, ci, co, cu.* By the time I got to *da, de, di, do, du,* I had it figured out. Only the first letter changed, and after that it was the same thing over and over. I didn't have to think about the letters on the page, or even look at them. So I started looking around. And listening. And I heard what the rest of the class was reciting:

A terrible beast is the bear,
He eats all who enter his lair.
Sharp is his claw, sharper still is his tooth,
He preys on the maiden and feasts on the youth.

Terrible? My bear was not terrible. She did have sharp claws and sharp teeth, but she never ate anyone. How could they say such bad things about a bear? I jumped up, dropping the book onto the floor. "That's a lie," I shouted. "What they're saying about the bear is a lie."

Mistress Dreiwatter stood up. "Come up here, Benno."

I stomped up to the front of the room.

"Turn around, face the class, and put both your hands on my desk."

I smacked my hands down across her desk.

"Go ahead and hit me. It's still a lie, what they said. I'll bet they've never even seen a bear."

She rapped me ten times across my knuckles. I stared straight ahead, as stiff as a soldier. Toad and Grub were laughing. Snort didn't laugh, he just twisted his mouth as if he'd seen something disgusting. Why didn't she hit them?

"Class, you will now sing 'Pity the Little Beggar Boy.'"

And the whole class stood up and sang,

Pity the little beggar boy,
He knows not right from wrong.
His life is hard, his days are dark,
He weeps the whole night long.

I thought maybe I should make up my own song, about wicked teachers and books that told lies.

When the song was over, Old Crack-Face put me on a high stool and held a sign from her desk in front of me.

"These words, Benno, say 'I Am a Donkey.'"

Then she hung the sign around my neck. I sat on the stool, wearing the sign, for the rest of the afternoon. Those were the only words I learned that day. And I knew those words probably weren't on the piece of paper.

Sitting on that stool, I had no work to do. So I watched the class while they did their work. Mostly, it was all the same—kids reciting or writing in their copybooks. But Snort and Toad and Grub were something different.

Watching them, I could see that Snort was smart. He did his sums and wrote his sentences really fast and, when he was done, he just sat and looked out the window. When the rest of the class was reciting, Snort never said a word. Until Mistress started walking toward his seat. Then he recited louder than anybody. And whenever she spoke to him, he looked at her as if she was a jam tart, and he smiled at her, and said, "Oh yes, Mistress Dreiwatter."

I could also see that Toad was just as dumb as Snort was smart. He sat next to Snort and kept poking him and then pointing to his own copybook, probably asking Snort how to do a sum or spell a sentence. So when Snort was finished—which was pretty quickly—he pushed his copybook over to Toad's side of the table, and Toad just copied Snort's work.

Grub wasn't as dumb as Toad or as smart as Snort. But he didn't like that he couldn't sit with them. So he kept twisting around, wanting to hear what they were saying, see what they were doing. And he did so much twisting around that he wasn't doing much work either.

The whole time I was watching them, I was trying to figure out why Old Crack-Face never took her stick to Toad or Grub. Their work wasn't any better than mine. And then, in the afternoon, Old Crack-Face called Toad up to her desk and asked to see his copybook. At first, her face was all sour, as if she thought he'd done all the work wrong. But it was Snort's work that Toad had copied, so all she said was "Your handwriting is deplorable, young man. You must practice." But she never raised her stick to him.

So now I'd figured it out. Toad and Grub took things for Snort, and in return he let them copy his work so they never got whipped.

But I wasn't learning to read. If I was going to do that, I'd better keep quiet.

But if I had to be quiet, I didn't have to be good. The next day, as Old Crack-Face was walking past my desk, I slipped the handkerchief out of her left sleeve and put it into her right. When she reached for the handkerchief, she didn't find it. She looked down and saw the handkerchief in her right sleeve. The lines around her mouth got tight, and she flicked three times. Next I started hiding the handkerchief. Once I put it under Snort's lunch bucket, once I hung it on the doorknob, and once I dropped the end of it into her inkwell. When she dragged it out, it dripped blue ink all over her desk.

She said she'd be watching me, that I couldn't fool her. Well, I was better at the work than anybody, and I had fooled her. I'd only been caught that one time, but I'd never be caught again. Certainly not by Old Crack-Face.

Every day I sat in the back with Niera, and she taught me the sounds of more letters. And every day after school, I took out the piece of paper and I tried to read it. But the letters still were nothing but sounds. They didn't make words for me.

EVERY NIGHT, Missus P. read me another story. She read stories about magic, about wizards and giants and trolls, about spells and secret words, about dragons that breathed fire and horses that could fly and fishes that could talk. She read about princesses locked up in towers and princes who had to do brave deeds. She helped me learn some of the words in the stories. And some of those words were on the piece of paper. I saw "fire," and "horse," and the words for numbers. I never knew that numbers could be written in letters. But I still couldn't make any sense of the note.

As the days crawled on, I started thinking terrible things. What if the zookeeper didn't take care of my bear, didn't feed her and clean up her droppings? What if there was no roof over her, to keep off the icy rain, the snow. Would she die? Was she already dead? And what if he *was* taking care of her, maybe then she'd get to like the zoo, and the zookeeper. Maybe she'd forget all about me. I had to find her soon, before she forgot me, before she died.

I'd been going to school for weeks, and I'd learned all my letters. I could figure out a lot of the words on the piece of paper. I could even put some of the words together, like "firehouse" and "horse trolley." But it still didn't make any sense. I would read a few words and then there'd be a word like "Hurtzlewerf." I needed help.

I was sitting with Niera on the bench at the back of the room.

"Niera, do you think you could read something for me?"

"Of course. What is it?"

"I don't have it here. It's at my house." I kept the note under my mattress, with the fresh bread I put in every day. "Could you come there with me, after school today? It's very important."

"What's it about?"

"I can't tell you now. I'll tell you when we get there. But you mustn't tell anyone."

I TOOK NIERA IN through the kitchen door. I was heading for the stairs, hoping that we'd get up to my room without Missus P. seeing us, but I hadn't counted on Missus P.'s ears. She came into the kitchen from the bakeshop.

"Hello, Benno. I see you've brought a friend."

She looked at me, as if she was expecting me to say something. What was I supposed to say?

"I'm Mrs. Pikche," she said, looking at Niera. "And you are?"

"Niera." She made a little dip with her leg and looked down at the floor.

"I'm pleased to meet you, Niera. Benno, there's bread and jam in the kitchen, and take some milk for the two of you."

Niera didn't say anything, just kept looking down. Why did Missus P. have to tell her that about the bread and jam? Now I had to give her some, and we'd have to sit and eat it. All I wanted was to have her read the note to me and go.

I cut some bread and slapped the crock of jam on the table.

I thought it would be faster if I just forgot about the milk. Niera nibbled at the bread with tiny white teeth, one little mouse bite at a time. Couldn't she eat any faster? Just stuff the whole slice in her mouth and swallow it down?

"Benno, could I have some milk, please?"

Oh, no! Milk, too. I poured it so fast, the milk splashed all over the table. Then I had to get a rag and wipe it up. More time wasted.

"Please, Benno, could I have another slice of bread?"

"Another one? I already gave you a slice."

"But there's a whole loaf, right here on the table. And this is a bakery. You can have all the bread you want."

"Don't you have bread at your house?" I was laughing at her now.

"Of course we do." Niera turned her head away.

I looked at her pale skin, her pointed chin, saw the sharp bones in her wrists, and I was sorry I'd laughed. I cut two more thick slices for her.

"I used to be hungry, too," I said, "until I came here." I'd never told that to anyone before.

Niera lifted her chin and looked straight at me. She had green eyes. "I'm not hungry! It's just that . . ."

"What? Just what?"

"It's just that . . . I have six brothers. They take big hunks of everything. My father, too. Afterward, there's not much left for me."

"Why don't you stand up to them? I saw you stand up to Old Crack-Face."

"Who?"

"Mistress Dreiwatter."

For the first time that afternoon, Niera smiled.

"You stood up to her that first day on the playground."

"Oh, Mistress likes me because she thinks I'm smart. But my brothers . . ." She was twisting her fingers. "My brothers don't think much of smart."

"I'll give you some more bread to take home," I said. "Don't let your brothers see it. But first you'll have to help me read something. Come on, I have it upstairs, in my room."

I pulled the note out from under the mattress.

"I can read a lot of the words, but then I get to this one, or this one, and I can't make any sense out of them. What do they say?"

"Those are street names. These are directions—they tell you to go three streets to Hurtzlewerf, then turn right two blocks, past the firehouse, to Pockenlager, then—"

"Stop a minute. You're saying that those words I couldn't read were street names? All right, I'll know the firehouse when I see it, but how will I know Hurtzlewerf Street or Pockenlager Street?"

"That's easy. You look for the street signs."

"Street signs?"

"They're fastened to the corners of buildings, at the end of every block. You don't understand, do you? I'll show you."

I raced ahead of her, out the kitchen door, down to the end of the block.

"Where? Where's the street sign?"

She pointed up at a sign fastened to the building.

"I've seen those, but I always thought they were shop signs, like all the others on the buildings."

"No, they're different from shop signs. The street signs are always this size and always have white letters on a dark blue background. And they're always right up here on the corner of the building, not over the shop window. See? That's the name of the street we're on, Hingle Street. And if you come around the corner, there's another sign with the name of this street."

"So all I have to do is look for those signs to tell me the names of the streets."

"Yes."

"Well, that's all right, then. I guess I'll see you in school tomorrow."

"Wait a minute. You said you'd tell me what this is about."

I thought for a bit. Niera never lied. If someone asked her, she might tell them.

"You promise you won't tell anyone."

"I promise."

"Spit over your shoulder three times."

Niera did that.

"These are the directions to my grandfather's house." I didn't know where my grandfather lived, or even if he was alive, but I said to her, "He's very old, and I wanted to visit him, but I couldn't read the directions he wrote for me. Thanks for helping me."

"I don't think that's right, Benno. Nobody lives in that place."

"How do you know that?"

"My oldest brother took me there last summer. No one lives there."

"Well, somebody lives there. My grandfather does."

"Not unless he lives in the zoo."

"The zoo? You've been to the zoo?"

"Yes, it's on the other side of the river."

"No, it's not. You're as bad as the rest of them. I've crossed the river on the Middle Bridge every day of my life. The zoo isn't there."

"Not the River Resier, the River Murin. There are two rivers in the city—the Resier, on the east, where we are, and the Murin, on the west."

There were two rivers and I didn't know it. I'd never gone all the way to the other river. This scrawny little mouse of a girl knew a lot of things

"You're going to the zoo to look for a bear, aren't you?"

"I am not!"

"Yes, you are. That day in school, you knew how to read the word 'bear,' and when the children were reciting 'A terrible beast is the bear,' you got really angry and said it was all a lie. Why do you care so much about a bear?"

I wasn't going to tell her. I hadn't told anyone since I'd come to the Pikches. But she was looking up at me, not down at the floor the way she usually did. She made me think of Pepi's mouse. Then I felt sad—for Pepi's mouse, for Pepi, for me. And sad for Niera.

"There's a bear in that zoo," I told her. "She's mine. I always took care of her. At least I did until they took her away."

Now Niera looked sad.

"Can I come with you? To the zoo? To see your bear?" she asked.

"Not this time. I—I've got to go by myself."

"But I know the way. I could take you there."

"She might be afraid of you. I just want to go by myself this time."

Niera looked straight at me, the way she had when she'd told me about her brothers.

"I'll tell you what," I said. "Let me see if my bear's all right. If she is, maybe I'll take you there some other time."

Then I ran back to the kitchen, took some currant buns, and gave them to Niera.

16

A Shadow

EVERY MORNING IN THE BAKERY, every day at school, every night in my bed, I saw the park. I could see the iron fence around it—all the parks had iron fences—but this fence was tall. It had to be tall or I was sure my bear would have already climbed over it and come to find me. The fence would have a gate, and when I came near, my bear would be clawing at it—the way she did every morning when she knew I was coming.

I could see her pushing her big furry head against mine, knocking me right down onto the ground. I'd laugh, and she'd grunt and lick me all over my face, so that I'd have to squinch my eyes shut. And then she'd lie down next to me, and I'd wrap my arms around her big neck and hold on to the rough warmness of her. And she'd chuff in her throat and I'd chuff inside.

I'd hardly slept at all the night before, waiting for that day, Sunday. No baking, no school. A whole day with my bear in her park.

"I'm going to see a friend tomorrow," I'd said to Officer and Missus P. They'd thought I meant Niera. "I'll be leaving pretty early, as soon as it's light."

"Don't you think that's too early to be visiting someone?" Missus P. had asked me.

"She knows I'm coming. She'll be waiting for me." I still hadn't answered Missus P.'s question. I'd have to make up a story. "Her brother made her a kite, and she's going to teach me to fly it. She says the wind is best in the early morning."

"Well, I'll leave a lunch for you, Benno. I think I'll make some sliced-meat sandwiches with pickled cucumbers. And those sugar cookies you like. And some oranges, because the sandwiches will make you thirsty. I'll make enough for your friend, too. If the two of you are getting such an early start, you'll soon be rather hungry."

Missus P. was always worrying that I might get hungry, but I was glad of it. I knew what hungry was.

I was awake and dressed while it was still dark out, and I sat in my room, in the chair by the window, waiting for the sun to come up. I kept hopping up, opening the window and peering out. Finally the sky began to lighten and I crept down to the kitchen.

Rrrow! It was Pum. I plucked him up and scratched his head.

"Not this morning, Pum. You stay here. Missus P. will be looking for you. I'll be back later. You wait here."

On the street, everything was gray—the sky, the shuttered houses, the bare trees—and still.

It was too dark to read the paper in my pocket, but I knew my way to the Middle Bridge. When I got there, the sky was turning to blue, and the river below shone right back. The air felt light and warm, like my feather bed. Spring was coming. The street sweepers, the milkmen, the night watchmen were trudging across the bridge, but I skipped around them.

When I got to the place where the bearded gentleman had written down the directions, I pulled them out. Me, Benno, reading directions. I looked around, hoping someone would see me reading, but no one did. At every corner, I pulled out the directions and read them again. I didn't want to make a mistake. Not this time. I found Hurtzlewerf Street and the firehouse and Pockenlager Street.

Next was the bridge over the River Murin. In my head, I'd been thinking of the Middle Bridge, but this bridge wasn't at all like that. It was only wide enough for people to cross on, not carts or carriages. The river wasn't wide, either, with no great ships, only small barges and canal boats. And across the bridge, there weren't any tall towers or domes, but the sun was glittering off something golden, something I couldn't yet make out.

No fine carriage horse could have run faster than I did across that bridge. And on the other side, it was there, the tall iron fence, the trees inside it, and the golden letters that spelled out ZOOLOGICAL PARK.

This wasn't like any park I'd ever seen before. It was so big it looked like it went on for miles. Finding my bear in there wasn't going to be easy.

The fence was as tall as two men. I yanked at the iron gate, but it wouldn't budge. It was straight bars all the way up, with spikes at the top, so I couldn't climb over it. A man inside was sweeping the gravel walk. He moved with quick, hopping steps, like a bird.

"Mister, isn't this the zoo?"

"It is."

"The bear, where's the bear?"

"Don't know anything about the animals, don't much like them myself. There might be a bear, don't know."

"Can you open the gate? I've got to get in."

"Not till it's time."

"When is that?"

"About an hour. Someone'll come and tell me, and I'll unlock the gate."

I couldn't wait an hour, I couldn't wait a minute. I ran along the fence. I ran until the sweeper was long out of sight. Then the fence turned a corner and I followed it. At the next corner, the fence became a brick wall. Now

I was on the opposite side of the park from where I'd started. A little farther on, by a pile of trash barrels, was a smaller, wooden gate. I pushed hard and it scritched open. I squeezed inside.

I was inside the brick wall, but it didn't look like I was still in the park. There were no trees, no grass. I had to find my way back. Then I heard an animal roar. A wild animal! They'd put my bear in a place with wild animals.

My belly started flopping like a fish. To my left, there was a stone building. I crept along to the end of the building. The roaring was getting louder. Ahead of me was a gravel path. I didn't know what might be out there. I could still run back, past the building, out the gate, over the bridge, back through the city, back to where I'd be safe. But if my bear was there, with the wild animal, I had to get her out, too.

Stepping softly so that my boots wouldn't crunch, I moved onto the gravel path. On both sides were stone buildings with bars across the front. Cages. Iron railings ran along both sides of the path, a few feet in front of the cages. There was an animal in each one. That's what a zoo was! It wasn't a park at all. It was stone cages with bars—like cells.

The roaring was coming from a cage to my left.

All right. Whatever animal was roaring, it was locked up in one of those cages. But where was my bear? Was she in the park? The one I'd seen through the iron gate? Or was she here in a cage?

Maybe they'd lied to me—Old Hookim and the zoo-keeper. Maybe they'd locked up my bear, just like they'd locked up Papa. A shivering fear crawled up my neck.

Someone was coming. A man with a heavy bucket in each hand had come out of a building at the far end of the path and was walking between the railing and the cages on my left. I didn't think he'd seen me. I ducked back around the stone building and peered out. The man stopped at a cage and opened a small door near the bottom. He poured something brown out of one bucket, then poured water out of the other one. He was feeding the animals. After he'd stopped at three or four cages, he turned around and walked back to the building he'd come out of, the empty buckets banging against his legs. But he'd be coming back to feed the animals in the other cages.

I ran behind the line of cages and came out at the far end. Now I was close to the building the man had gone into. I waited until he came out with two more heavy buckets. As he walked along the line of cages, I crept along behind him. He never saw me—no one ever did.

He passed the first cage, where he'd left the food and water, and went on to the next. Why was the man going so slowly? Cage by cage, I followed him. When he'd passed each cage, I looked into it. Then I looked across the gravel walk to the cages opposite. A lion. An elephant. A zebra. We were near the end. Maybe my bear wasn't here after all.

The next-to-last cage looked empty. Why had he left food and water in an empty cage? But no! The cage wasn't empty. There was something dark in there, in the far corner. Something that didn't stir. Something that didn't make a sound. Something—that might be dead.

I didn't want to look at it.

But I couldn't turn away. As if a rope was slowly pulling me, I stepped up to the bars. The floor of the cage was higher than the ground, just even with my knees. A cloud covered the sun, throwing the inside of the cage into shadow. I squinted my eyes. There was a shape in the corner, a dark shape, large and still. What was it? It couldn't be an animal. Not even a ripple of breath lifted its ribs.

No, it wasn't an animal. It was just a pile of manure in the corner of an empty cage. That was all. Just a pile of manure. I started toward the next cage.

Whuuuh . . . A sound, like a low, deep breath, came from the back of the cage, from that dark shape.

My own breath stopped. I turned back, and as I looked, one end of the shape lifted an inch or two from the cage floor, then dropped back. Her round ears! That was my bear's head!

I grabbed the cage door and shook it.

"Bear! Wake up! It's me, Benno."

She didn't move. Didn't she hear me? Why didn't she open her eyes, come to me?

"Please, Bear, wake up. I know you're only sleeping. Wake up, please, you're scaring me."

"Get back from there! Get back from that cage!"

I spun around.

The man with the buckets was a few yards away, facing me, and I saw that he was the zookeeper, the one who'd taken my bear away. He dropped his buckets and ran toward me.

"I know what you're up to, sneaking in here to tease and torment that poor dying animal. Get away from there, this minute!"

"What's wrong with my bear? Why doesn't she move? Why doesn't she come to me?"

"Your bear?" The zookeeper came closer. He stared at my face, looked down at my clothes, then back at my face again. "Oh, you're the boy from the courthouse. I didn't recognize you at first."

"Get away from me!" I screamed at him.

"Boy, there's nothing you can—" He stepped between me and the cage.

"I said, get away!"

I was punching his skinny chest and kicking his legs and crying all at the same time.

"All right now, son. Quiet down, I'll get back."

I turned to my bear, but my eyes were clouded up with tears. I stood there, holding the bars, not even able to see her. Then, from above me, I heard a pigeon cooing.

"Do you hear that, Bear? Do you hear the pigeon?

Remember how we listened to the pigeons that last morning? Listen, can you hear it?" And I coughed away the tears in my throat and cooed to her.

Just then the cloud drifted off and sunlight flooded the cage. I could see my bear clearly. She turned her ears toward me and opened her eyes. But her eyes looked like marbles, like stone-blind marbles.

Over my shoulder, I hissed at the zookeeper, "You did this to her. You said she'd be in a park, with trees and grass. You lied to me. You put her in a cage and now she's sick. She doesn't even know me."

He stepped up beside me and looked into the cage.

"I don't know what's wrong with her. She won't eat. I've been feeding her, twice a day. See, there's food in her cage right now. For a while she took a little water, but now she won't even do that."

My bear's beautiful, warm eyes were cold, empty. I stretched out my arms between the bars, trying to touch her. She lifted her head, then dropped it to the floor of the cage and closed her eyes again.

"It's no use, boy. She wants to die—she's starving herself. There's nothing we can do for her now. I know it's hard, boy, to see an animal just give up like that. Let her be."

"I won't let her be. I won't let her die. What is it, Bear? Why won't you eat?"

She needed to eat. She'd eat if I fed her. I took one of the oranges Missus P. had given me, and began pulling it apart. A sweet, sharp smell burst out of the peel. My bear raised her head again and sniffed the air. She pawed the floor of the cage with one front leg, pulled her leg under her, and tried to stand. But she was too weak. She sank down, her legs folded under her.

I held out the pieces of orange to her, pushing my arm through the iron bars until they cut into my shoulder.

"Eat it, Bear. This is for you, you can eat it." She wouldn't take any food unless I told her to eat. "Eat the orange, Bear. It's for you."

Slowly she rolled herself onto one side and stretched one front leg out. Then she rolled a little onto her other side and stretched the other leg out. Pulling from one front leg to the other, she dragged her shaking body along the floor of her cage. After a few feet, she dropped on her side and closed her eyes. I could see her ribs and hips sticking out like kindling wood.

She was too weak to crawl to the orange. Then the orange would have to go to her. I took out a second orange and rolled it along the floor of her cage. But she moved her leg as the orange came toward her, knocking it to one side.

I was still holding the pieces of orange. I tossed them to her gently, one piece at a time, so they landed beside her head. She slid her mouth toward the orange pieces and, without lifting her head from the floor, licked each one into her mouth. Slowly, slowly, with her head on the ground, as if every bite was hurting her, she ate them.

She didn't make a sound, eating that orange. No snuffing or snorting, no smacking her lips. But she did eat it.

When she'd finished, I took out another orange, peeled it, and threw the pieces to her. I was about to peel another when the zookeeper put his hand on my arm.

"No more for now, son. Too much food at once wouldn't be good for her."

My bear laid her head on the floor of the cage, and she seemed to be sleeping. But in a few minutes, she lifted her head and tried to roll from her side back onto her belly. Several times she fell back, but finally she heaved herself up and began dragging herself toward me again.

Pressing my whole body against the bars, I stretched my arm as far as it would go into the cage.

"That's it, Bear. You can do it. You're a good bear, you can do it."

She was only inches away from me. I could feel her warm breath on my hand. But she couldn't crawl those last few inches. She lay with her head on the floor of the cage, her eyes turned up to me, panting.

The bars were squeezing my shoulder like a carpenter's vise.

"It's all right. You rest now, Bear. Rest a little first, then you'll make it."

She closed her eyes, and I took my arm out from between the bars and waited.

The zookeeper moved up beside me. "Boy," he said

softly, "I think she used up every last bit of strength she had, just crawling those few feet. Best thing would be for you to go on home now. I'll tend to her."

"Didn't you see? She wanted to come to me. Unlock her cage so I can go in there with her."

"Afraid I can't do that. I shouldn't even allow you to be inside the railing. If anyone saw you here, you'd be thrown right out of the zoo. And I'd lose my job."

"Then I'll wait. She'll come to me. I know she will. She only needs to rest first."

She lay very still, just like before. But after a while she opened her eyes and looked at me. I reached out to her again.

"That's it, Bear. You're nearly here. Just a little bit more. You can do it."

She had to stop once more and rest, but then she made it all the way to my hand, and she licked it.

I pushed the basin of water closer to her. She lifted her head a little and drank, making lapping noises with her tongue. Then she dropped her head to the floor and rolled her eyes toward me.

"You did fine, Bear, just fine. I'll stay, I won't leave you."

"Boy, the zoo will be opening soon. If anyone sees you standing there, with your arm through the bars of the bear's cage, there'll be the devil to pay."

"I'm not leaving her."

"You don't have to leave. Just stand back behind the

railing, like all the other visitors." He pulled a watch out of his pocket. "It's time. They'll be coming in pretty soon."

After a while a little boy came along the path with his mama and papa, a little fancy boy tied up with a big bow in the front.

"What's that, Mama?"

"That's a bear, my darling."

"Why isn't he doing anything, Mama? I want him to do something. Wake up, bear! Wake up! Mama, the bear won't wake up."

The fancy little boy started to cry. Good. I didn't even have to pinch him.

"Come along, my precious. Leave the poor old bear alone. We'll go and look at the lion."

My bear lay very still, so most people, when they came to her cage, looked in and walked on past.

When no one was around, me and the zookeeper fed her the last of the oranges. The zookeeper wouldn't let me go near the cage again, in case someone saw, but I gave him the food, and he put it into the cage for my bear. She was still lying where she'd dragged herself, close to the bars, and she didn't have to move at all to reach the food. But she'd open her eyes and look at me and turn her ears to listen to me. Then I'd say, "Eat it, Bear. It's good food, you eat it." And she'd eat.

After the oranges, we fed her the sugar cookies. I could hear them crackling in her mouth, and her lips made smacking noises. When all the oranges and cookies were gone, I gave the zookeeper one of the sandwiches.

"I think that'll be too hard on her stomach," he said. "Let's just try the bread."

When she'd eaten the bread, she licked up the crumbs from the floor. I ate the meat and the pickled cucumbers.

"It's late, boy. The zoo'll be closing soon. You'll have to leave."

"But my bear—I have to stay with her. She won't eat unless I'm here."

"You can come back tomorrow. She's had enough food for the first day. And look at her, look how much better she is. She's holding her head up and she's more awake. It'll be dark soon, and she needs to sleep."

Dark! I had to get back.

"Bear, listen to me. I have to go now, but I'm coming back tomorrow."

My bear turned her ears toward me.

"It's just like before, when I'd put you in your pen at night and you'd sleep there, and then I'd come back in the morning."

I turned to the zookeeper. "Please, let me touch her before I go. There's no one here now, everyone's gone. I just want to touch her head and then I'll go."

The zookeeper looked around. The gravel path was empty.

"All right, but be quick."

I ducked under the railing, and in two steps I was at the

cage with my arm through the bars. As I reached out to touch her, my bear lifted her head and licked my fingers.

"You've go to go now, boy. Let her rest."

I took my hand out from between the bars, then put it back one last time and scratched my bear behind one ear. I wasn't sure, but I thought I heard her humming.

IT WAS NEARLY DARK when I walked into the kitchen. Missus P. was standing at the stove, Pum rubbing against her legs. Officer P. was loading firewood into the oven, getting it ready for Monday morning's baking. Suddenly I was too tired to stand and dropped onto the bench by the bake oven.

"We were worried, Benno. You were gone so long. Where were you?"

I didn't answer. I didn't want to even look at him, but Officer P. sat down next to me, took my face in his hand, and turned me to him.

"What's wrong, Benno?" he asked. "You're trembling."

"You lied to me!" I shouted.

"Lied to you? How?"

"You said my bear was going to a park. She wasn't in a park. She was in a cage. They never once let her out. And she didn't eat the whole time she was there. Her bones . . . She couldn't walk, couldn't even stand. She didn't know me, her eyes . . ."

"Benno," Officer P. broke in, "I didn't know. I was sure your bear was fine. Believe me, Benno, I didn't know."

He tried to put his arm around my shoulders, but I shrugged him away.

"You knew she wasn't in any park. You knew she was in a cage."

"Yes, but Benno, they take good care of the animals at the zoo. They . . ."

Officer P. and Missus P. looked like people made of wax. Missus P. sat down on the other side of me.

"Benno," she said, "I can't believe they didn't feed your bear."

"They did feed her. But she wouldn't eat. I always brought her her food. Even when she was a cub, I . . ."

"Benno." Missus P.'s voice was as quiet as Niera's. "Benno, if she won't eat, I'm afraid . . ." She reached for my hand, and I let her take it.

"But she did eat. When *I* gave her the food. I broke open one of the oranges. And the smell of it . . . She tried to crawl to the orange, but she couldn't do it. So I threw the pieces to her. And the sugar cookies. And the bread."

"Did she eat them, Benno?" Missus P.'s waxy face was turning back to pink.

"Yes. She ate it all. And then she crawled on her belly and licked my hand." I looked down at my hand, and I could feel her warm, wet tongue licking it. "I have to go tomorrow and feed her. If I don't, she'll die."

"You'll have to go after school, then, Benno"—Missus P.'s voice was strong again—"and feed your bear."

"I told her I'd come in the morning. She'll be waiting for me. Why do I have to go to school? Why can't I just go and be with my bear?"

Officer P. said, "Benno, you know very well what Magistrate Hookim's orders were. If you don't go to school, I'll have to report it to him. If he sends you away, you certainly won't be able to see your bear."

"Benno, did she like the bread?" Missus P. asked.

I nodded.

"The cookies were sweet. Bears like sweet things," said Missus P. "Why don't we, when we're baking every morning, make two extra loaves for your bear. We'll make her sweet breads, glazed with honey."

I couldn't speak. I just nodded my head.

Officer P. walked over to the money box, counted out a fistful of coins, and put them into my hands.

"Here, Benno. When you go to the zoo, take the horse trolley. You'll get there faster. And home faster, too. When you need more, just ask me."

Why did he have to go and do that? I'd been keeping my eye on that money box. All day the woman kept the box under the counter in the bakery, and every time she sold a bread or some buns, she put the money into the box. At night she carried it into the kitchen. On Saturdays, when Mustache came home, he took his pay out of an envelope and put that money into the box, too. When I was ready, I was going to take it all.

But now Officer P.'d just given me money, told me to ask for more when I needed it. And Missus P. was going to bake bread for my bear. I wouldn't have to steal it from the kitchen or hide it under my mattress.

It was all upside down.

17
Always a Thief

I WAS WHISTLING ALL THE WAY. Whistling and throwing my book bag into the air and jumping up to touch the leaves on the trees. This was the last day of school, the last day I would ever have to look at Mistress Dreiwatter. After today, she'd be alone all summer, sitting behind her high desk in the dusty classroom, her fingers curling around her wicked stick, wishing she had me there to thrash.

But me, I was going to have long, long days just doing things I liked—helping with the baking in the early mornings, reading stories together in the evenings—and all day long, all the long, warm summer days, being with my bear.

She'd been getting stronger every day, and fatter than she'd ever been, what with the sweet breads Missus P. and me baked for her and the food the zookeeper brought her. I was always the one to feed her, though, because she would only eat if I gave her the food. The zookeeper told me that all morning she paced back and forth in her cage, wouldn't eat anything that he put into her basin. But, he said, when it was time for me to come, she'd stop pacing and stand at the bars, looking for me. As I ran down the gravel path to her cage, I could see her muzzle sticking out. When I got close to her cage, I could see the muscles in her shoulders trembling with excitement.

I had to stand outside the railing, but she'd look straight at me and I'd say to her, softly, "I'm here, Bear. Go on, eat your food."

She'd gobble everything in her basin. Afterward she'd raise her head and sniff the honey breads I was keeping in my pockets.

"Not now, Bear. The breads are for later," I'd tell her.

When the zoo was closing, and all the visitors had left, the zookeeper let me go under the railing, right up to my bear's cage. My bear would lower her head and sniff my pockets.

"What is it, Bear? Looking for something?"

I'd pull out the breads, one at a time, and hold them through the bars. She'd grab them right out of my hand with her teeth and set them down on the floor of her cage. But she didn't eat the breads right away. She knew that in a few minutes I'd have to leave her. While I was still there, she wanted to lick my hands, have me scratch her behind her ears, and listen to me talk to her. The breads were for later, after I'd gone.

On Sundays, I had a whole day to spend with my bear, and sometimes I took Niera to see her. Niera always brought a pocketful of sweets. She'd give the sweets to me, and the bear would take them from my hand, humming as she sucked them down. Once, I let Niera touch my bear's neck. Niera laughed and said the fur tickled her. My bear's fur was growing heavier, covering her skin and bones thickly. Her fur was soft again and darker, too—not dusty-looking the way it had been, but brown like the apples Missus P. baked into her cakes.

In school that last day, I was supposed to be reciting from the reading book with the class, but I didn't like the story. It was about a boy who always did bad things, like hitting other children and dropping a kitten down a well, so his good mama turned into a wicked witch and left him forever. I stopped reciting. After a while the voices of the other kids sounded to me like my bear humming. I started thinking about my bear. Three times Mistress Dreiwatter told me to stop smiling and pay attention, and she hit me with her stick. Then, when I didn't tell her what six times twelve was, she made me sit on the donkey stool. I didn't care. Soon I'd be rid of her forever.

"Class"—Mistress Dreiwatter rapped her stick across her desk—"please come up, one row at a time, and place your books and copybooks in straight piles on my desk."

When that was done, she asked us all to lift the lids of our tables and clean out any refuse that we found there. One of the girls walked up and down the aisles with a trash can. Mostly, people threw away pencil stubs too short to write with and scraps of paper that they'd been passing notes on. But when Grub lifted the lid of our table, he pulled out of a back corner something that was left from an old lunch—it was covered with gray fur and looked like a dead mouse. Maybe that's what he ate.

When Grub threw the dead-mouse lunch into the trash can, the girl screamed and dropped the can. The whole class came running over to see what had happened, and Mistress had to rap her stick on her desk for a long time before everyone quieted down.

At last the day was over, and we all stood up and said together, "Good-bye, Mistress Dreiwatter." I was shouting louder than anybody. Suddenly the cracks in her face got deeper. She was pushing papers and books all over the desk, and one pile of books crashed to the floor.

She pulled herself straight. "Class, no one will leave this room. My purse is missing." Her voice was like an icicle. "The thief is in this room, and he will return my purse immediately."

Everyone was still.

"Children, take your seats. The girls may leave, but the boys shall remain."

The girls stood up and hurried out, but I could see Niera, beside the doorway, waiting for me.

One at a time, Mistress called the boys up to her desk

and asked each one if he had taken her purse. Finally the only ones left were me and Snort.

"Petrolin, did you take my purse?"

"Oh, certainly not, Mistress. I would never do such a thing."

"Do you know who did take it, Petrolin?"

Snort looked sideways at me. "I really couldn't say, Mistress." He smirked.

"Thank you, Petrolin. You have been most helpful. You may go now."

"Good-bye, Mistress Dreiwatter. Have a pleasant summer. And I certainly hope you catch the culprit who stole your purse."

"Thank you, Petrolin. I know I shall."

Snort turned to go. Old Crack-Face had her back to him, and he stuck out his tongue at me.

Mistress Dreiwatter stood up behind her desk, picked up her stick, and stared at me. Her eyes sliced right down into my gut.

"Stand up, Benno."

I stood up next to my table.

"Up here, if you please. Beside my desk."

I walked up to her desk.

"Return what you stole from me this moment."

"I never stole anything from you."

"Benno, you were arrested for stealing, were you not?"

My mouth dropped open, but I couldn't say a word. It

didn't matter to her that I'd learned to read, that I was good at sums. She only knew that I used to steal things.

"Answer me, Benno. Were you not arrested and sent to live with Officer Pikche as your punishment?"

"The Pikches don't punish me. I haven't stolen anything from them."

"You are not only a thief, you are incorrigible as well. Turn out your pockets."

I stuck my hands into my pockets and turned them out. My knife and a shiny rock clattered to the floor. A piece of string and the pocket handkerchief Missus P. made me take to school didn't make a sound.

"You must have hidden the purse somewhere. Where is it? Turn around, Benno."

When I turned around, she began thrashing me across my back. I stayed perfectly still.

Now Niera rushed back in. "Please, Mistress, Benno didn't do it. You mustn't thrash him."

"Mustn't? Do you presume to tell me what I may do?"

"Beg pardon, Mistress. I only meant that—Benno is my friend. I know he didn't steal your purse."

"Niera, Benno is not a fit companion for you. Please leave us."

"But Mistress . . ." Niera was angry, talking loud, the first time I'd ever heard her speak out in school. "Benno was sitting with me today. He was never near your desk."

"Niera, leave this room immediately."

Mistress Dreiwatter raised her stick at her.

Niera looked down at the floor and left the room.

"Benno, if I cannot get the truth out of you, there is someone who can. Magistrate Hookim has the right punishment for you. Return to the Pikches and wait there. I shall come presently and have Officer Pikche place you under arrest."

Suddenly I was back in the courtroom. I saw Papa, punching and kicking. I felt my bear beside me, trembling. This time Magistrate Hookim would lock me up for sure. And then my bear would starve to death.

When I got home and found Pum sleeping in the sun outside the kitchen door, a plan came to me. The plan was risky, but I had to try. When Pum saw me, he stretched and yawned and blinked his yellow eyes.

"Wait here for me, Pum. I'll be right out."

I grabbed an empty flour sack from the pile in the corner of the kitchen and stuffed the two loaves of bread for my bear into my pockets. Outside, Pum was still lying in his patch of sun.

"I'm sorry about this, Pum, I really am."

Pum seemed to know what I had in mind. He loved to be picked up, and usually he went all soft and curled right into my arm. Not now. When he saw the sack, he jumped to his feet, ready to run. I grabbed him, but he stuck all four legs out stiff as wood. Trying to stuff Pum into the sack was like trying to put an armload of kindling into a lady's purse. Every time I got the sack open and tried to put it over Pum's head, he'd squirm his neck and twist his whole body around until I had to drop the sack and use both hands just to hold him.

I finally did manage to get the opening of the sack over his head. The only thing I could do then was turn the sack over and drop him into it.

"I'm sorry, Pum. I know you don't understand."

Pum was even sorrier. All the way on the horse trolley, he clawed at the sack and made the most terrible yowling noises. The other passengers were all staring.

"Supper. I caught it myself," I said, and smiled like the sun. People stepped to the other side of the trolley.

Pum's yowling was making it hard for me to think. I had a plan, but I worried that something would go wrong. What if my bear attacked Pum? What if Pum ran away?

Those things were too terrible to think about.

At the zoo, no one was standing outside my bear's cage. She was at the bars, waiting for me. But when she saw the wriggling sack and heard the yowling, she slunk back into a far corner. I put the sack on the ground, opened it a little, just enough for Pum to poke his head out. Then I pulled one loaf of bread out of my pocket, held it in front of Pum, and threw it into my bear's cage. Pum wasn't looking at the bear in the corner. He only cared about the bread. I opened the sack wider, and Pum leaped out and squeezed between the bars after that bread.

My bear reared up on her hind legs and began raking the air with her long, white claws, blowing and clacking her teeth. Now Pum raised his back, all the hairs on his body and tail standing straight up, and let out a long, long shriek. My bear whumped down her front paws and started to moan—low, then up high, then low again.

The shrieking and the moaning brought people running from all over.

Someone started screaming, "There's a cat in the cage! There's a cat in the bear's cage!"

I could tell now that my bear wasn't going to hurt Pum, but Pum didn't know that. Even so, Pum didn't run away, but stared with round yellow eyes straight at my bear, his back up and his fur sticking out. He kept on shrieking. Pum was a brave cat.

The zookeeper ran up. "What's going on here? What's all the commotion?"

"It's my cat. I had him in a sack, but he escaped and ran into my bear's cage. I can get him out of there."

"Benno, why on earth did you bring a cat in here? Now look at the trouble you've caused."

"I know, I'm sorry. I thought my cat would like to see my bear. But I forgot that Pum loves bread just as much as my bear does. When I threw the bread into the cage, Pum just leaped in after it."

"Well, Benno, you've made a real mess of things. Now I'm going to have to try to coax the cat out of there."

"Oh, but he'd never go to you. Look how frightened he is. He'd come to me, though. Can't I get him?"

All the while I'd been talking to the zookeeper, I had my fingers in his pockets, feeling for his keys. When I found them, I carefully slid them out and hid them up my sleeve.

"All right, everybody. The cat belongs to this boy here, and he's going to try to get him out. Everyone stand back."

I ducked under the railing and stood in front of the door of the cage, close in so that no one could see what I was doing. I held on to the bars with my left hand and, with my right, slipped the keys out of my sleeve and tried one in the lock. It didn't fit. Neither did the next. I didn't have much time. But the third one fit. I unlocked the cage door and left it closed. From the far corner, my bear had been watching me. Now she began padding toward me. Pum suddenly got quiet.

Then people started screaming again, "Watch out, the bear's going to attack! Get back from that cage! Someone pull that boy away from there!"

"Pum, come on out of there," I called. "Come on, come back out of the cage."

What with the bear coming closer and all the people screaming, Pum's bravery finally quit on him. He turned around and leaped out between the bars, back into my arms. When Pum was safely in the flour sack, I climbed back under the railing and went up to the zookeeper.

He turned toward the crowd. "All right, folks. It's all over now. Quiet down and let this bear eat her supper."

The zookeeper looked at me angrily. "Benno, I can't imagine why you would do such a foolish thing. That cat's probably lost four or five of its lives. As for your poor bear—I think you'd best take your cat home now, before he tears that sack to shreds and runs away."

While the zookeeper was scolding me, he was petting Pum through the sack, trying to quiet him. I slipped the keys back into his pocket.

"You're right. I really am sorry. I wasn't thinking too well. Here's the other loaf of bread for my bear. Would you give it to her, please? I'm going to take my cat home now."

On the trolley, Pum just lay curled up and quiet inside the sack. I had to peek in a few times to make sure he was still alive. I didn't know if he was quiet because he'd worn himself out or because he knew he was going home. Anyway, the sack was a lot easier to hold. I loosened the string just enough for me to slip two fingers in and scratch his head.

"Thank you, Pum," I said. "You're a brave and good cat."

Inside the kitchen door, Pum jumped out of the sack and shook himself all over. He began to lick his fur, just as if nothing had happened. I was glad he couldn't talk.

"Is that you, Benno?" Missus P. came in from the bakery. Her eyes looked blurry, and her skin was very pink.

"Sit down, Benno." She sat down on the bench, and I sat down next to her. She looked at me for a long time. Then she said, "Mistress Dreiwatter has been here."

"She told you I stole her purse, didn't she? I hate her."

"No, Benno. You don't hate her."

"I do. She hates me, and I hate her even more. She lied. I didn't steal her purse. But I bet I know who did."

"What do you mean, Benno?"

"Nothing."

"Mistress Dreiwatter has asked that Officer Pikche arrest you and bring you before Magistrate Hookim."

"He'll send me to that place for wailing youths."

"Benno, if you know who stole the purse, tell me. We want to help you."

"You can't help me. When she tells Old Hookim that I stole her purse, who do you think he'll believe? Not me!"

"Benno, Mistress has accused you, but she has no proof."

"What do you mean?"

"I asked her if she saw you take the purse or if you'd had anything that was taken from it. She said she hadn't seen you take it, nor did you have anything from it."

"That won't matter to Old Hookim. Hookim won't believe me. He believes people like us—like Papa and me—need to be locked away. First Papa, then my bear. I'm next."

"No, Benno. Not if you're innocent."

I couldn't listen anymore. I ran up to my room and lay down. Pum pushed the door open and sprang onto the bed. He settled down on my chest, looking at me with his yellow eyes. I stroked his neck.

"You never stay mad at me, do you, Pum? You're not

mad at me for stuffing you into the sack, for tricking you into my bear's cage, not for anything. If Old Crack-Face were a cat, she wouldn't stay mad at me. And then I wouldn't have all this trouble."

Pum just blinked at me.

IT WAS GETTING DARK when Officer P. came into my room.

"Mrs. P. told me what happened. We both believe you're telling the truth, son. But I'm afraid I've got to report Mistress Dreiwatter's accusations to Magistrate Hookim. She wants me to arrest you, but I won't do that. I'll explain to Magistrate Hookim that you've done nothing wrong the whole time you've been with us. Except the time you didn't go to school. But I don't need to tell him about that, since you've gone every day since."

Well, I thought to myself, now I'll never have to go to school again.

"I'll tell him how you've learned to read and how you help out in the bakery. Don't you worry, I'll get everything straightened out. Come down now and eat your supper. In the morning, I'll get it all straightened out."

I didn't eat much supper. I didn't even want any raisin cake for dessert. And after supper, I didn't want to listen to a story. I went back up to my room and lay on the bed with my clothes on. I heard their voices in the kitchen, heard them climb the stairs to their room. I waited till the whole house was quiet. Then I got out of bed and pulled the feather bed up over the pillow, the way Missus P. had showed me to do in the mornings. I took my knife out of the drawer and put it in my pocket. All my clothes were folded, smelling of fresh ironing. I shut the drawer—Officer P. had fixed it so that it didn't stick anymore—and I crept down to the kitchen.

I took a piece of paper and a pencil and wrote a note. The writing was hard. I didn't know how to spell all of the words. But I hunched over the table and did the best I could.

I didnt take the perse. Thats the truth. But no one will beleeve me. Exept you. And Niera. This is the best plase I have ever been in my life and I wish I cud stay here. But I cant becawse I know Old Hookim is going to lok me away.

Your frend,

Benno

While I was writing the note, Pum sat next to me, watching. I added one more thing at the end.

Pum beleeves me too.

When I was done, I stood up, and Pum tried to climb up my leg. I scooped him up, and he rubbed his mouth against my cheek and licked my chin with his rough tongue. I put him down softly.

The moonlight was shining through the kitchen window, onto the kitchen shelf, onto the money box. Lying next to the money box was the book of fairy tales.

I lifted the lid of the box. The coins inside gleamed in the moonlight—crowns, half crowns, and coppers. I thought how Papa could use that money. He could buy food and coal for his cookstove. He'd have enough money to last him for weeks. I could take all the money out of the box, wrap it up safely, and run back to the Stalls. I'd put it in Papa's room so he'd have it when he came home from prison. I reached into the box, took a handful of coins. And then I saw Officer P. holding out a fistful of coins to me. For the trolley. I put the money back.

Then I reached for the storybook and put it inside my jacket.

18
Escape

"THIS IS THE LAST TROLLEY tonight, boy." The driver stretched and yawned. "You sure you want to go all the way out there? There won't be a trolley back."

"I won't be needing a trolley back. I'm spending the night with the zookeeper. He's my uncle."

"All right, then, climb aboard."

The last stop was just before the footbridge.

"You take care, boy."

I ran off, my feet pounding on the wooden bridge, the storybook pounding against my chest, my head pounding. I'm coming, Bear, I'm coming.

The zoo was closed for the night, but the gate in the back was never locked. As I dashed to the line of cages, I heard footsteps crunching toward me along the gravel path. I crouched down in the shadow of the wall of the first cage and waited. A circle of light swayed from side to side, shining into the dark cages. A man carrying a lantern walked past me—no more than two paces away. The light from the lantern hit the ground in front of me. I flattened myself against the wall, holding my breath. Then the man turned and walked back the way he had come.

As the footsteps moved farther off, I crept out onto the path. At the far end was the building where the zookeeper kept food for the animals. A square of yellow opened up and then closed into blackness. I guessed that the man with the lantern had gone inside. But he might come out again. I had to hurry.

The gravel path shone white in the moonlight. In the distance, my bear's cage was a black shadow. When I came near it, my bear pushed her muzzle through the bars and grunted.

"Wait, Bear," I whispered. "I'm going to let you out."

I pulled hard on the cage door, but it didn't open. What was wrong? Had the zookeeper locked it again? I felt a drumming in my head and chest. My bear began whimpering. I knew she wanted me to take my hands away from the bars of the door and stroke her.

"Quiet, Bear," I whispered, pulling harder.

It was no use, the cage door didn't budge. Even my bear pushing against the bars didn't budge it.

Pushing! That was it! I'd been trying to pull the cage door open when maybe I needed to push it. But my bear had grown heavy, and I couldn't open the door against her weight.

"Get back, Bear. Back."

She did as I told her, turned around, and padded to the straw in the corner of her cage. I pushed with all my strength—but I'd gotten too strong. The door swung open and struck the side of the cage with a loud *clang*. I leaped in after it and closed the door behind me.

A crack of yellow opened in the food building and grew wider. I huddled behind my bear on her straw. Footsteps came toward us, and the light from the lantern traveled down the path. When it reached our cage, the light made a large, slow circle around the inside of it.

The lantern moved away, down the line of cages, making more slow circles, then along the other side, and back to the building. The door closed again, and we were in darkness.

My bear pushed her head against my cheek, and I wound my arms around her neck, burying my face in her fur. She twisted her nose to my hand, sniffing, looking for a loaf of bread, a sweet. I hadn't brought her anything! I still had no wits about me! I'd taken the storybook for me, but I hadn't taken anything for her. My ribs ached with sadness.

"I'm sorry, Bear, I'm so sorry. Come with me now. I'll find us some food, I promise."

My bear started licking my face. I could tell that she wanted me much more than she wanted a sweet. That made me ache even worse.

With my bear next to me, I crept toward the door and quietly pulled it open. But when I stepped down, my bear moved back and lay on her bed of straw.

"Let's go, Bear," I whispered. "There's no time. Hurry."

I looked over my shoulder down the path. The door of the building was still closed.

"Follow me, Bear. Quickly now."

But my bear wouldn't move. Then I realized that every night of her life, she had slept locked up—in a pen at the Stalls, a cell in the police station, a cage here at the zoo. At night, when she was alone, her cage was like a blanket that she wrapped around herself. She thought that tonight would be like every other night.

I climbed back in, put my arms around her neck, and pulled. "Please, Bear, you've got to come with me. I know you don't understand what's happening, but I'm going to make everything right. Come with me, come now."

My bear knew the word "come." Papa had trained her well. She got to her feet and, with my arms tight around her neck, padded to the door.

I looked quickly toward the building.

"*Come*, Bear," I whispered. "*Come* now."

She stepped down out of her cage, and when I jumped over the railing, she jumped after me. Her big paws scattered gravel everywhere, with a sound like heavy rain, but the door stayed shut.

Outside the zoo, my bear stopped, looked around, and

started to walk toward the city. She could find her way anywhere, and I saw that now she was going to find her way back to the Stalls.

"No, Bear, no. Not that way. Come with me."

She turned and looked at me. Then the two of us walked together, just the way we used to walk to the market, my hand on her neck, her head rolling from side to side, her front paws turning in. But this time I wasn't holding the end of a chain.

Once before I'd been out in the darkness, going to a place I didn't know, the night Officer Pikche had taken me home. That night I was shaking with fear and cold, and I'd wanted my bear with me. Tonight I had my bear with me and the night was warm, but still I was shaking with fear.

I led my bear away from the zoo, away from the city, following a dirt road, pebbly and rough, with only the moon for light. The dirt road became a path, soft under our feet. In the months since I'd found my bear at the zoo, she'd grown fatter, but I'd grown taller. Her head didn't quite reach my shoulder anymore.

We walked on and on, the moon dropping lower. It still lightened the sky above, but straight ahead, a wall of darkness shut out the moonlight. We stopped, and I held tight to my bear. We couldn't turn back. Where would we go?

Now my bear rose up on her hind legs. She took deep gulps of air, her head up, her nostrils quivering. Then she lowered her front paws and began to walk toward the darkness.

As she pulled away from me, I felt dizzy, as if I was falling from a very high place.

"No, Bear, no. We can't go there."

But the bear kept on walking.

"Stop, Bear. Stay where you are." I was crying. She knew those words. Why wasn't she listening to me?

I wished I had the chain and could pull it tight and hold her back. But I wouldn't have been strong enough to hold her. No one would have been. I ran after her.

On both sides of us, tall trees rose up, shutting out the moonlight. I stayed close to her. My throat was dry, but my body was dripping sweat. My eyes were growing used to the dark, but there was little to see. The sky was gray above the black trees. The ground was black, too. Then a wind came up and blew apart the branches, making a path for the moonlight.

My bear was putting her paws down slowly and carefully, as if she wasn't sure where to step. After a while she stopped and scratched the ground. She sniffed the earth and then stood quietly, listening, looking. Every few steps, she stopped to claw the ground, the bark of trees, even the rocks—to listen, to look.

My legs were stiff and aching, but my bear kept walking faster and faster, then broke into a run. I tried to run after her, but I tripped over rocks and fallen branches.

"Please, Bear," I called. "Please, I can't go on." Shaking,

I dropped to the ground. Dried leaves and twigs crackled under me. Above me, I heard a *hoo-hoo-hoooo*. My bear ran on.

I tried to call out, but fear had made my voice small. She was too far for me to see her in the darkness. At first I could hear her heavy footsteps, moving away. Then there was nothing. And then I heard *thud, thud, thud* rushing toward me. Was it my bear? Or was it something else, something coming to kill me? No matter what it was, I couldn't run.

The thudding came close, and then I felt a warm breath on my face. My bear sniffed my face and my body.

"I can't walk any more tonight, Bear. Please, we have to find a place to sleep."

Leaning against her shoulders, I pulled myself up, then stumbled along beside her as she walked on. Soon the ground grew pillowy under our feet. She stopped, circled, and lay down. I bent down and felt the ground. She'd found a bed of moss, our bed for the night. I flopped down beside her.

The cool night air dried the sweat from my skin, chilling me. I moved closer to her. She began to push at me with the soft leathery cushions of her heavy paws, chuffing softly. Then the chuffing turned to snoring, and she was asleep. I lay on the moss, next to her, and listened to the night sounds of the forest.

Although I was very tired, I couldn't sleep. I thought about the note I'd written. I was proud of that note. I'd never written one before. I said the words over and over to myself. But then I started to think that I'd left out some things.

I'd left out that I didn't take any of my new clothes, except for the ones I was wearing. And I didn't write that I'd taken the storybook. Would they be mad? Would they say that was stealing? They believed that I didn't steal the purse, but now they'd have to tell Old Hookim that I'd stolen the storybook. So he'd send me to that place anyway.

Or he would if he could catch me. But I wasn't going to let that happen.

19

The Forest

APALE LIGHT BROKE THROUGH THE TREES and
woke me. My bear was gone—I was alone. I jumped
to my feet.

"Bear! Bear! Where are you?" I called. "Where did
you go?"

I turned in a frightened circle, looking for her. I saw
her a few feet away, sitting in a clump of bushes behind
me, curling her tongue around the branches and peeling
off the red berries. Her eyes were half-closed with happiness. She didn't even chew the berries, just peeled them
off and swallowed them.

I was suddenly hungry, too. I pulled off a handful of
the berries and started to chew. Phfew! I spit them out.
They were sour! I looked around and found some black-
ish berries on another bush. I plucked off a handful and
brought them back to my bear. If she ate them, I guessed

they'd be safe. They might be sour, but they wouldn't be poisonous. She licked those berries right out of my hand, then followed me back to my bush. I pulled off a berry and tried it. It was sweet. I guessed that when my bear could choose, she liked sweet berries better than sour ones.

We ate every berry off the bush, but my bear got a lot more than I did. When the bush was picked clean, she walked over to a sunny space and padded through the tall grass. She walked in a circle, sniffing at the grass, until she found a clump that pleased her. Then she sat down, half closed her eyes again, and began tearing at the grass, chewing it noisily. I wasn't hungry enough to eat grass, but if I stayed in the forest, I might have to.

Overhead, the sun was getting stronger, making lacy patches on the forest floor. We walked deeper into the trees. Sometimes my bear sniffed at a rock and then, with her strong claws, pulled it up and rolled it away. Underneath, on the soft, wet earth, she found beetles, ants, and slugs, and scooped them up with her tongue. Other times she'd find a rotting tree trunk, tear it apart, and suck up the white, crawling bugs inside. Afterward she'd lick her lips, smacking them together, just as if she'd eaten a sugar cookie. One time she turned over a rock and slammed her big paw down on a little brown mouse.

I really needed to find some more berries. I surely wasn't going to eat bugs or mice.

In a little while my bear broke into a trot, and I had to run to keep up with her. The ground became rocky and sloping. She stopped running, lifted her head, and listened. I heard it, too, the splash of rushing water. She saw it first and then I did—a fast-flowing river, breaking and bursting over rocks. She dashed ahead of me. When I caught up to her, she was standing in the water, with sunlight skipping all around her.

She cocked her head to one side. Then she pushed her nose down, blowing bubbles. She lifted her head out and shook it, spraying the drops of water into the air. Then she pushed her nose down once again. She seemed to be looking for something. She clawed the water, still looking, then started walking toward the bank where I was standing. But instead of coming to me, she stopped in a shallow pool among the rocks, rose up on her hind legs, and rammed her front paws down. She ducked her head under the water, and when she brought it up again, she had a sparkling, silver fish in her mouth. She shook her head wildly from side to side and swallowed the fish in one gulp.

Fish! Now there was something I could eat. Missus P. sometimes cooked a fish for supper, frying it in a big iron skillet. I could almost taste it, the brown crispy outside, the sweet and white inside. I took off my clothes and waded in the water next to my bear. I tried to catch one of the silvery fish in my hands, but I didn't have my bear's big, leathery paws or her sharp claws. The fish just slipped away.

My bear'd been eating fish after fish, but she stopped now and watched me. The next fish she caught, she didn't eat. Instead, she tossed it up onto the bank. She'd caught the fish for me!

I scrabbled up to where the fish had landed. It was flopping over and over, still alive. I felt kind of bad for the fish and thought about throwing it back into the water. But then I remembered the mouse and the bugs, and I knew I'd rather eat the fish. I waited until it had stopped moving. I took out my pocketknife. The skin felt slimy, not crispy, the way it was when Missus P. had cooked it, so I cut it off. Then I pulled away the bones. I'd never eaten raw fish before. But I decided to do what my bear had done with the sour berries—take a large gulp and swallow it down. It came right back up. Along with a lot of berries. Raw fish sure didn't taste like cooked fish.

Well, if I wasn't going to starve to death I'd have to learn to eat my fish raw. I ate the rest slower, chewing it a lot before I swallowed. It tasted slimy, the way the skin had felt, but this time it stayed down.

My bear kept on catching fish and eating them while they flopped from her teeth. Finally she climbed up onto the flat rock where I was sitting. The sun warmed the rock and put us both to sleep.

When I woke up, the sun was low, and I was alone. I ran up the bank, calling. I found her in a grove of pine trees that stretched like feathers into the sky and filled me with their sharp, clean smell. Stripes of sunlight slanted to the ground, and the earth was thick and soft with fallen pine needles.

. . . This mushroom grows under pine trees, and its flesh is as sweet as the smell of the pines.

I could hear Papa's voice, but I couldn't see him clearly. His face was blurred behind the red beard. I could see the mushrooms, taste their sweetness, but I couldn't see Papa. Even when I closed my eyes, all I could see was his thick fingers slicing through the stems.

What would Papa do when he came home to the Stalls and didn't find me there? Would he be angry? Would he shout or kick? Or would he be sad that I was never coming back? The way he was sad that he could never go back to his village.

A strange sound, like a hoarse trumpet, came from not far away. My eyes flew open, and I jumped to my feet. My bear was standing up on her hind legs, just the way she used to do when she danced to Papa's concertina. Only she wasn't dancing now. She was standing very still with her head high. She made the trumpet sound again. As I watched her, the setting sun turned her fur to gold—just like the bear in the story. Only she was better. She wasn't wearing a suit of gold under her fur, her fur *was* the gold.

That night, we made the pine grove our home. I took off all my clothes and piled rocks together to hide them in, with my storybook in the middle, so they wouldn't get spoiled if it rained. Those were the first fine clothes I'd ever had, and I didn't want them to get torn or soiled. And I surely wouldn't need my boots. I'd always gone barefoot in the summer, and the soles of my feet got as hard as horses' hooves. It felt funny, being naked outside, but I liked it. Until the sun went down and a strong breeze came up. Then I dug out my underdrawers and put them back on.

My bear with her claws and me with my hands heaped up a big bed of pine needles. Every night after that, no matter where we went in the forest, we came back to the pine grove to sleep.

Except when it rained. When it rained, we crawled under a rock ledge and slept there. After the rain, when the earth smelled dark and cloudy, we could find mushrooms. My bear knew the good mushrooms as well as Papa, and she huffed and snorted as she swallowed them down.

On days when the sun shone, the berries ripened to red and blue and black, and we ate them all. Once, in the late afternoon, while I was picking berries and my bear was licking them off the bushes, I started to whistle, a tune that Papa used to play on his concertina. When I looked over at my bear, she was standing on her hind legs, turning slowly around, dancing. I quickly stopped whistling. Then I started to cry—big, gulping gasping sobs. My bear lowered her paws to the ground, came over to me, and began licking my face.

"It's all right, Bear. I don't know why I'm crying."

And I didn't know why. Was I crying for the bear? Or for Papa and me?

When we got back to our pine grove, I took my book out of the pile of rocks and opened it to the story of the bear. When my bear came over and began sniffing the book curiously, I started to read the story aloud to her.

Then a funny thing happened. I was reading the words aloud, but it was Missus P.'s voice I heard. And I felt as if Officer P. was sitting next to me. By the time I got to the end of the story, the light was nearly gone.

I WANTED US TO FORGET THE CITY, but the city came to us. The first time, we were playing in the shallow water near the bank of the river. I'd found an empty turtle shell, and I was filling it with water to take a drink, when my bear came splashing up to me and swatted the shell out of my hands. Then she caught it in her mouth, tossed it into the air, and swam after it. She kept doing that, tossing the shell and swimming after it. I couldn't swim, but when she tossed it back toward me, I caught it and threw it back to her. She liked that, and pretty soon we were splashing around, tossing the shell back and forth.

I was laughing and my bear was leaping around, when suddenly she stood up tall, lifted her head, and listened. At first everything seemed quiet. Then I heard sounds. But not the sounds I'd grown used to in the forest. They were sounds I knew from another place—the sounds of men's voices. I couldn't hear what they were saying, but I knew what they were doing. They were looking for me and my bear. And I knew they'd find us. Signs of my bear were everywhere. Her heavy paws left deep footprints wherever she walked. She rubbed her back against the trees, leaving patches of fur, and she stood up tall and made deep claw marks in the bark.

The voices were still far away. We could run. But where could we run that they wouldn't find us? We had to go where there would be no sign of us.

My bear was standing tall in the water, listening to the men's voices, smelling their scent. Very softly I called to her.

"Bear, come here. Come to me."

I was close to the shore, closer to the men who frightened her, but my bear swam back to me. In the shallow water, she put her four paws down, and shaking with fear, I grabbbed her around her neck and climbed on. Her back felt broad and strong under me. My bear knew what we needed to do. I couldn't swim, but she could. She swung around in the water and, walking at first, then swimming as the water got deeper, she headed for the other side of the river.

I couldn't get my arms all the way around her thick neck, so, with my head pressed against the back of her head, I clutched her fur and dug my knees into her sides. Her front paws moved like oars through the rushing water, and I could feel the muscles in her shoulders tightening and pulling. When we got to the other bank, I climbed off her back, my arms and legs aching.

On this side of the river, the trees came right down to

the edge of the water. I flattened myself under the trees and lay still to watch and listen, but I knew that my bear would be seen.

"Go on, Bear. Go."

This time she obeyed me and quickly disappeared into the deep forest. I lay still for a long time, and then I saw them, first heads, then shoulders, then five or six men coming toward the river. The sound of the rushing water swallowed their voices, but some of their words carried across the stream.

"... footprints ... bear ..."

"... other side ..."

"... can't swim ..." That voice was Officer P.'s—so he was looking for me, too.

The men's voices were quieter now. They were talking among themselves. I couldn't make out the words, but from time to time I heard Officer P.'s voice. Once I thought I heard him saying, "Come on, son. You've braved the storm this far. You can make it. I'll help you."

But he couldn't have said that. I must have imagined it.

As I watched, some of the men started upstream, the others went downstream. When I couldn't see them any-more, I turned to find my bear in the forest. I couldn't risk calling her—I'd have to look for her.

There was no path through the forest on this side of the river. The trees grew thickly together, shutting out the sun. It was the best place for my bear to hide, her dark fur disappearing into the darkness, such a deep darkness,

I'd never be able to see her. But I was sure that no matter how far she'd gone, she'd sniff my scent, hear my footsteps, and she'd find me.

I tried to follow her, but half-buried rocks smashed my toes, and sharp thorns tore at my bare skin. I went back to the bank and flattened myself on the ground. All day I waited, not daring to move. My belly was grinding with hunger, my throat aching with thirst, but I made up stories to make the time pass. Those stories weren't like the ones in my book. They were about me.

In one story, Officer P. found me and told me that Mistress Dreiwatter was dead and would never bother me again. And I went back to live with the Pikches and Pum. I fell asleep thinking about that story.

When I woke up, I made up another story. In this one, Papa was on the other side of the stream, looking for me. When he found me, he pulled me against his chest, and I told him everything that had happened. Then Papa told me not to worry anymore. He took me and the bear back to his village, where everyone welcomed us, and we all lived happily ever after.

I didn't know which story I liked better. I tried, but I couldn't make up a story with everyone together.

When dusk came, the men gathered at the place where we had crossed the river. They talked for a while, then went back the way they had come. As soon as they left, my bear appeared beside me. Had she been nearby all along, watching them?

That night, we crossed back. I ran to our pine grove and pulled apart the piled-up rocks. They hadn't found my clothes, but I knew they'd return, so I hid the clothes again. In the morning, I stuffed myself with as many berries as I could find. They weren't much, but they'd have to last me the whole day. Toward midmorning, my bear heard them coming. Before we crossed, I wiped out our footprints in the mud.

Just like the day before, I lay on the opposite bank, hungry, thirsty, and alone. The men came back for two more days, but they never crossed the river, and then they gave up looking.

After the men stopped coming, my bear and me were happy again, playing in the water, eating berries and mushrooms and fish, sleeping in our pine grove. Once, very early in the morning, a deer bounded into the grove. It was prettier than the deer in my school primer, with great brown eyes, legs as thin as reeds, and spiky antlers. I wanted him to stay, but when he saw my bear he bounded away. Smaller animals came, too, even a fox, but they all ran away when they saw the bear.

Then, one morning, when I woke up, the deer had come back. He was standing at the edge of the grove, one leg lifted as though ready to run, but he didn't move. Didn't he see my bear? Wasn't he afraid of her? But my bear wasn't in the grove. She'd probably gone off to find food—these days, she was eating all day long and getting fatter every day. As I got up to look for her, the deer ran off.

"Bear? Where are you, Bear? Come on back and we'll eat together."

But my bear didn't come. Where was she? Had something happened to her?

I ran down toward the river, calling as loudly as I could. As I waded into the water, she came out of the dark forest on the other side, stood for a moment on her hind legs, then plunged into the water and swam back to me.

Most mornings, when I woke up, my bear was next to me. But when she wasn't, I knew that she'd gone across the water, where I couldn't follow her, and into the forest. Sometimes when I called to her, she didn't come right away but stayed across the water, deep in the forest. She began to stay away longer and longer.

Whenever I was alone, I thought about how the summer would end, how the fish would be gone, and the berries and the mushrooms, and the rain would turn to snow. The zookeeper had told me that when winter comes and its food is gone, a bear in the wild just goes into a deep sleep and waits for spring. My bear wouldn't feel hunger or cold. But I would, and I would die here even before the winter came.

My bear belonged in the forest. But I didn't. I had to go. Back to the city, back to Papa. It had been six months since they'd sent Papa to prison. In another month, he'd be coming back. I had to go back, too—without my bear.

One night it rained—not a soft, summer rain but a cold, hard rain. My bear and me crawled under a rock ledge, and I lay shivering next to her. The side of me that touched my bear was warm, but the side away from her was cold.

I hardly slept that night. When the sky began to turn from black to gray, my bear stirred and stretched. I leaned toward her and kissed the flat place on her head. She licked my face, and we started down toward the river.

Along the way, my bear stopped to lick the ripe berries and chomp the fresh mushrooms. I watched her, but I felt too sick to eat. When we reached the river, she plunged into the water and began catching fish. She tossed one up on the bank for me. I looked at that fish, flopping in the grass, and remembered our first day in the forest. My bear was watching me. I had to eat that fish—she'd caught it for me. My throat hurt so much, I could hardly swallow. I ate one small piece and, when my bear's head was in the water, threw the rest of the fish away.

When she'd eaten her fill, my bear climbed onto the bank and lay down in the sun to sleep. But when I started back to our pine grove, she got to her feet and followed me. I pulled away the stones, put on my clothes, and tucked the storybook into my jacket. My bear knew those clothes—they belonged to the city, not the forest. She backed away a few steps and began to scream, *uh-waaa, uh-waaa, uh-waaa*—like the scream she made when she first came to us, the scream I was feeling inside.

I didn't want it to be like this. I wanted my bear and me to be together always, the way it was in my story.

My bear was still screaming.

"Come with me, Bear. I want to show you something."

I led her down to the bank of the river and with a sharp stick, I scratched the word "Bear" in the soft earth.

"See, Bear? That's your name."

My bear looked down at what I'd written. Then she looked up at me.

"And this," I said, scratching "Benno" beside her name, "is mine."

Then, with my foot, I wiped out all the letters. I put my arm across my bear's neck, and we walked back to the pine grove.

MY CLOTHES FELT STRANGE, stiff and tight, not soft and warm, like the first time I had put them on. Caught inside the boots, my toes couldn't grip the ground. I pulled off my cap and stuffed it into my pocket.

I started toward the path, my bear walking beside me, her head turned up to me, her eyes fixed on my face. My hand was on her shoulder, heavy now with fat and muscle, her fur thick and soft. She didn't stop to strip the berries off the bushes, she didn't lower her head to tear at the grass, she didn't claw at the rocks to suck out the insects beneath. She walked slowly beside me, watching me, only once in a while screaming softly, *uh-waaa, uh-waaa.*

We kept on together until we reached the edge of the forest. Then she stopped, raised her head, and looked down the dirt road, the road that led back to the city.

"Good-bye, Bear," I said. "You were the best friend I ever had in my life."

My bear's brown eyes were fixed on my face. "And I was your best friend, too. That's why I brought you here. And that's why I have to leave you here."

No, I thought, there's something more I have to tell her.

"Bear," I said, "you aren't my blood—not like Papa is—but you are my family."

My bear licked my face. Then she watched as I walked away.

Every few steps, I stopped and looked back at her. She grew smaller and smaller, still watching me, and then I couldn't see her anymore. But even after I couldn't see her, even when she couldn't see me, I knew she could still hear my footsteps, smell my scent. And she'd stay still, looking down the dirt road, until there was no more sound or scent of me.

I was going back to the city without my bear. I'd never again rush out of our room in the morning to give her her food, comb her, and sit beside her to watch the pigeons. I'd never again lie on my mat at night, feeling the place on my cheek where she'd last licked me. My chest started to feel like a cart horse had stepped on it.

20

Rumitch

IT WAS VERY LATE when I walked back into the Stalls. I'd waited until long after dark, when everyone would be asleep, the boys not playing in the street, the old people not sitting outside. Even in the dark, I remembered the way to my bear's pen, in the corner below the stairs.

The lock had been broken off or stolen, and the pen was stuffed with rotting garbage and rusting cans. The stink of it twisted in my belly, choking me. I felt for the rusty, broken shovel, took it off its nail, and, from outside the pen, beat at the wooden boards until they lay in a splintered heap and covered the rotting mess. I threw the shovel on top and climbed the stairs.

My nose and eyes were burning with tears. I could hardly see and had to pick my way along the crooked hall. I knew Papa wouldn't be in our room—he would be in prison for another month. But I needed a place to stay.

I'd live in our room until Papa came home. No one would be looking for me anymore.

But our room was locked shut. I ran back down the stairs and pounded on Old Man Rumitch's door.

"Who's there?"

"It's me, Benno."

There was a scraping and a clanking as Rumitch undid the locks and peered at me over the chain.

"Benno? What are you doing here? Your papa's still in prison."

"Why is our room locked? I can't get in."

"The bailiff came and sold all your belongings to pay the court fine. Everything but the stove—that wasn't worth selling. Then the landlord rented the room to some new people. What are you doing here, Benno? I thought they sent you to live with the policeman."

"I need a place to sleep. Can I come in?"

Old Man Rumitch waited for a moment and then undid the chain. Day and night, his room was dark—he kept only one candle burning. He pulled me up to the light and looked at me. I smelled dust and mold. His skin and hair and even his clothes were the color of ashes.

"You ran away, didn't you? What did you steal from them? Have you brought me something of value?"

"I didn't steal anything! I have nothing for you!"

"What's that inside your jacket?"

He grabbed my jacket in his bony fingers and pulled out the storybook before I could snatch it back.

He turned the book over in his skinny hands. "You stole this, didn't you? Pheh, it's worth nothing to me." He shoved it back against my chest.

Rumitch was quiet for a minute, watching me. "You'll need a place to stay. You can stay here," he said. "But this isn't the poorhouse. You'll have to pay for your keep."

"How can I pay? I haven't any money."

"Eh, you still have your fingers, don't you? Fingers like a spider? You've gotten a little stouter, I see. Taller, too. But not too big to work. What do you say, do you want to stay here?"

"How can I work without my bear, without Papa?"

"Sometimes a boy can work better alone. What do you say? Do you want to sleep here or on the street?"

I said nothing.

He went to the stove, spooned a thin broth into a bowl, and gave it to me with an end of bread.

"Thank you."

"Quite the little gentleman, you are now. 'Thank you.' And you've a little gentleman's clothes now, too. That may be all to the good. I've an idea how you can work. I'll tell you about it in the morning."

Rumitch showed me a corner where I could sleep. The night was hot, but I felt cold. I lay there, needing my bear beside me. Once, in the deepest part of the night, I woke up suddenly and thought, I'll go back. In the morning, I'll go back to the forest.

But when morning came, I knew I couldn't do that.

When I left the Stalls, Pepi and Mohno were playing ball in the street.

"Benno, you're back." Pepi caught the ball and started to walk alongside me. "Where's your bear? Did you see? Someone smashed in her cage last night."

"I know. It was me."

"Why'd you do that? Where'll you put your bear now?"

Mohno came running up. "Aah," he said, "his bear's got a cage in the zoo. He's never getting his bear back. Come on, Pepi, throw me the ball."

"My bear's not in the zoo!" I walked faster. "She's not in a cage either."

"Yeah, she is," Mohno said, grinning. "Your papa's in prison and your bear's in the zoo. Everyone here knows that. Come on, Pepi. Throw me the ball."

I whirled around. "My bear's not in the zoo, and she's never going to be in a cage again. If you don't believe me, go to the zoo and see for yourself."

"I just might do that." Mohno snickered. "'Cause if there's an empty cage at the zoo, they'll have to put you in it."

I punched Mohno hard, right on his sneering mouth. He staggered back, holding his face in his hands.

"No fair! I'm bleeding!"

"I'd punch you again, crybaby, but I haven't got time to waste."

Old Man Rumitch had told me to go to the West Station, where the trains went out of the country. He'd said to find the first-class section, because the people there had the most money. I was glad I didn't have to work in any of the markets. Someone there might remember me. I might even see—No, I didn't ever want to see him again. I knew he'd have to arrest me. But I thought I'd even rather go to jail than hear him say, "I thought you were a good boy, Benno. I must have been wrong." And then he'd have to tell Missus P. about me.

The West Station looked like a castle in my storybook. It had towers that nearly touched the clouds. The roof was covered in tiles of every color, and there were a thousand windows, pointed at the top, with panes of glass in purple and gold. The station was so long the street went through the middle of it, with a doorway tall enough for a horse trolley to drive right in.

I'd walked by the station many times, but I'd never been inside. The crowds were much greater than in the market. Noise and traffic—every kind of carriage and cart and van, so jammed together, not one could move—and drivers shouting and cursing. Rumitch was right, this was not a place for a bear. But I could squeeze my way through.

The station inside was just as mad as outside. Porters were pushing wooden carts, piled high with trunks and bags and boxes, vendors were singing out their wares— pastries and drinks, newspapers and magazines. Mamas in fancy hats were towing their children along while the papas staggered behind with carpetbags and lunch baskets.

I pushed my way to the first-class platform. It was

almost like being in the forest again. A forest where iron trees stretched their branches across the tracks. I read the signs and found the place for the first-class cars. With my proper-boy clothes, no one shooed me away.

I did what Rumitch told me. I waited until the passengers were getting ready to board the train. In the fuss of porters and bags and such, no one was watching me. But I was watching them. I saw right away that this wasn't like the market. The ladies had dainty little purses that dangled from their lacy gloved fingers, but there wasn't any money in those purses. When a lady wanted to buy something—a lemonade or a packet of peppermints—she asked the gentleman to pay for it. And then the gentleman pulled out a fat purse and counted out the coins. The gentlemen were easy. They were always keeping one eye on the porter, to make sure he didn't go wandering off but put their bags into the right compartment. I saw right away that the porters would be my look-aways. My fingers were quivering and my feet were happy. I was working again.

By late in the afternoon, I'd emptied quite a few purses and tossed them away. But I was very hungry. I'd eaten little since yesterday morning, when I left the forest. Rumitch's broth had been mostly water with some bits of potato and onion and a few grains of barley. But that was last night, when I'd come to him with nothing but my storybook, which he didn't even want. Tonight, when I emptied all the money onto Rumitch's table, there'd be a fine supper.

But there wasn't. Rumitch ran his bony fingers over all

the coins, scraped them into a box, and locked the box in his tall black cabinet. "Tonight," he said, "there will be something extra for your supper, Benno." He spooned out the same thin broth, but he did drop a soup bone into it. And he gave me two slices of bread and a sweet to suck on afterward.

I'd been working at the West Station for about a week, growing hungrier every day, when I suddenly realized I had money for food—the money I was bringing home to Rumitch each night. I bought fruits and little cakes and sweet drinks—everything the vendors had to offer.

When I emptied my pockets onto Rumitch's table, he was not pleased. "Eh, this is all you got today? Five coppers, and a lady's bracelet? And the bracelet is only glass. A man with two fingers could bring me more than you do, Benno. This will not even pay for your supper and the candle you burn late into the night."

That night, there was only one slice of bread for me, and the bowl of broth was only half-full. But I didn't care—I knew I'd eat my fill at the West Station.

It wasn't only my belly I was filling. There were things at the train station to fill my head as well. In the main hall, between the food vendors, there were book stalls. I didn't dare to take a book. Even though I looked like a proper boy, the booksellers kept their eyes on me. But I read the names of the books over and over—*The Castle of Ordheim, Lost at Sea, The Hunt for Hidden Treasure*—imagining the wonderful stories inside.

And even if I couldn't read the stories, I could read the newspapers that people left behind on benches. Pretty soon, I was spending the days eating fruit and pastries and reading newspapers. I only did enough work to buy food for myself and bring home a few coins for Rumitch—only enough so he'd let me stay.

I read all sorts of things in the newspapers. I read about a Dr. Livingstone, who'd gone off to explore a jungle in a place called Africa. He'd disappeared three years before, and someone had just found him. I never could have lived in the forest for three years. I wondered how he'd done it. He didn't even have a bear to help him.

Before I could read, I hadn't even known about the River Murin, but now I was reading about a country called Prussia and another country called France. Those two countries were fighting a war. And then one day, I read something in the newspaper that was as wonderful as any story in a book. In that country of France, there was a city called Paris. When the war came, people escaped from the city in *balloons*. Not little balloons, like the ones they sold in the parks in summer, but great big ones, with baskets hanging from them for people to stand in. I read that story over and over.

But little by little, something was twisting around in me. One day, as I was dipping my fingers into a purse, I heard a voice. It was Officer P., and he was saying to me, "Stealing is a crime." I quickly pulled my fingers out of the purse and looked behind me. He wasn't there.

I tried another purse, but this time, instead of the open purse, I saw Officer P.'s mustache, the corners turning down, the way they did when he thought I'd done something bad.

All that day, something was the matter. I didn't feel glad to be doing my work. My feet felt like stones, my fingers like wood. My eyes and ears weren't sharp.

I only wanted the day to be over. That night, when I sat silent at Rumitch's, eating his thin broth and bread, I remembered how it was at the Pikches. Not just the good food, but Pum hooking his bread and all of us talking and laughing.

After supper, when I read my book at Rumitch's table, close to the candle, I remembered being settled down under my feather bed, with the lamplight turning my white room to yellow.

Every night at Rumitch's, I read my storybook. And I always finished with the story of the golden bear. I knew parts of it without even looking at the words, especially the end.

. . . the bear's rough coat suddenly fell off, and there stood a tall man, dressed entirely in gold.

"I am a king's son," he said. "The wicked dwarf, who stole all my treasures, forced me to wander about in this forest in the form of a bear until he died. Now he has got his punishment."

When Rumitch put out the candle, I'd tell myself over again the stories in my book and the stories in the newspaper. And then I'd think about the books at school. Not the primers. At the back of the room, there had been a whole shelf of real books. When we'd finished our lessons, we could choose a book from the shelf.

At first, I wasn't able to read the books at all. Even later on, the books were hard for me. But toward the end I was leaping from book to book, trying to read them all at once—*A Natural History of the World, The Book of Wonders,* and *Fables.* But of them all, my favorite was *Fearless Tomi, Dog of the Alps.* I needed to read more books. I could feel it in my belly—like being hungry.

THE LONG DAYS rolled into longer weeks. But Papa's time in prison would soon be over, and I knew everything would be different when he came home.

The autumn sun burned in the sky, and the station, with its coal-fired train engines and its clouds of steam, was an oven. The men in third-class were in their shirtsleeves, but the gentlemen in first-class kept their coats on. They tipped back their straw hats and mopped their brows with white handkerchiefs, but they never took off their coats.

One day I was standing on the platform, thinking that it would be easier to work the third-class section, where there weren't any fancy coats hiding the men's pockets. Then, not three feet away from me, a gentleman reached inside his coat and pulled a gold watch out of his vest pocket. I knew that watch. I knew that gentleman. I remembered the fur on his winter overcoat, the softness of his clothes. I could still hear him calling, "Stop, thief!" I could hear the angry crowd, feel myself wrenching free, running, turning, see my bear fall to the ground, bleeding. And then I saw Papa being led out of the courtroom in shackles.

I ran from the station all the way to the Stalls and pounded on Rumitch's door.

When he let me in, I threw three coppers onto the table.

"Here, Rumitch, this is all I got today."

Rumitch said nothing, staring at the three coppers. Then he looked up at me and smiled, a strange, secret smile.

"Why are you looking at me like that?" I shouted. "Are you expecting more? There is no more. It's no good. I can't do the work."

"I can see that." Rumitch sneered. He said nothing else but kept on looking at me with that same mocking smile.

"I said, I can't do the work. And I won't, ever again."

"Do you think I need your work?" asked Rumitch, turning toward the cabinet to put away the three coppers. "I only kept you here as a favor to your papa." He locked up the coppers and turned back to me. The smile had faded from his face. I knew then that he was going to put me out on the street.

For the first time since I'd run from the station, I thought about what lay ahead. I'd have no place to live, no food, no money. A terrible fear took hold of me, like the fear I'd felt that night I'd followed my bear into the forest.

But just like that night, I couldn't turn back now. Rumitch would have let me stay if I'd asked him, if I'd promised to do the work again. But I never would.

"I won't do the work anymore. I want to be free of it."

I stepped to the table, picked up my book, and started for the door.

"You're a fool, Benno," Rumitch said from behind me. "But you're not my fool any longer. Your papa's back. He'll beat some sense into you."

Suddenly, I felt as if I was in the middle of the rushing river, hanging on to my bear's neck—with the men on the bank behind, coming to take me away, and on the bank ahead, a dark place I had never been. Only now I didn't have my bear to hold on to.

"Where is Papa? He can't be in our old room. Where is he?"

Rumitch's mouth tightened. "Your papa's on the ground floor. The third from the front."

As I ran out, Rumitch called after me, "You and your papa owe me the first week's rent. With interest."

21
Chalk-Dust Days

I STOOD AT THE DOOR, outside Papa's room, staring at the cracks in the dirty, gray wood. The last time I'd seen Papa, he was in shackles, being led away to prison. Would he still be angry at me? I opened the door slowly.

The room was empty, except for an old, rusty stove, a chair with a broken back, and two torn bed mats. A long time ago these rooms on the ground floor had been the horse stalls. Three of the walls were stone, with one small window in the back wall. The dirt of the floor was packed so hard it was like stone, too.

Papa couldn't be living here, I thought. Rumitch must be wrong.

I was about to leave when the door banged open. A man stood in the doorway holding a bundle of scrap wood, the daylight from behind him putting his face in shadow. The man was thin, his shoulders bent.

"I—I'm sorry. I thought this was my papa's room. I'll get out," I said, moving toward the door.

"Benno."

The voice sounded old, dusty. But something in it was Papa's. I started to shake.

This wasn't the Papa I remembered. His skin looked like the skin of an old peach, dull brown and wrinkled. His hair and beard had faded.

I took the bundle of wood from his arms and put it next to the stove. When I turned back, Papa was shuffling toward the chair. He dropped into it heavily and with the fingers of one hand drew me to him.

Months before, when I'd seen that dead shape in the empty cage at the zoo, I'd felt as if a rope was pulling me toward it. Now a rope was pulling me toward Papa.

"Papa . . ." I stood over him. Papa's hair hung in thin strands to his shoulders. His shaking hands clutched my arms.

"Benno. You've grown taller. And not so skinny."

"They gave me lots of good food, Papa. Meat and fresh bread. Missus P. even made cakes and tarts—"

Papa was scowling. "For seven months, they starved me. They boiled a potato in water and called it soup. What they called bread was like a brick."

"I didn't know, Papa. I thought . . ." But I hadn't thought. I'd thought about my bear, saved food for her at first, then brought her bread every day. I'd never thought that Papa was starving.

"There were twenty of us—sometimes more—all locked together. It was always cold in the prison, even in summer, and dark. When they led me out into the sunlight, it was the first time I had felt warm in seven months. But my eyes had grown weak in the darkness."

Papa held out his arms, his empty hands facing up.

"Benno, they took everything from us. They even smashed the bear's pen. We'll have to find boards, nails, wire, build a new one. When we take the bear from the zoo, she'll have to have a pen."

Papa pounded his fists against his legs. "We'll take back the bear, we'll work again, and we'll buy the food we need."

Papa hadn't even raised his hand to me, but I felt as though I'd been struck. The bear hadn't been only mine. She'd belonged to Papa, too.

"Papa, the bear is not in the zoo. I took her out of there."

"You took her from the zoo? You stole her away from the zoo? Good. We'll build a pen, get a new chain, you'll show me where she is, and we'll bring her back." For a moment Papa was the old Papa again, strong and straight.

"No, Papa. She's free now. I took her to the forest."

He pulled into himself, like a drawer shutting. "We need the bear, Benno. Without her, we will starve." He didn't look at me.

Why hadn't I taken the money from the box? I should have taken it for Papa. But I hadn't. Instead of the money, I took the book, for me. I could never change what

I'd done—but I could do things differently from now on.

"We won't starve, Papa. I'll work, we'll have money."

"Yes." Papa opened himself up again. "Rumitch said he's taught you to work without the bear." He gave me a hard look. "Rumitch said, in the beginning, you did well, but lately you haven't been bringing him much." Papa brought his face close to mine. "Rumitch is a good man, Benno. He even paid the week's rent for our room. You should have worked harder for him. But now you will— you'll work the way he taught you. We'll pay Rumitch back for the rent and the interest. We'll get back our old room."

I started to say *Yes, Papa,* but the words stuck in my throat. I looked away. In my mind, I was seeing the railroad station, the crowds, the porters, and the gentleman with the fur-collared overcoat and the gold watch.

"No, Papa. I can't." I looked back at him. "I can't do the work anymore. Papa, I saw the gentleman today, at the train station. The one with the gold watch. I was so afraid I ran, just like before. Papa, you've been in prison. If they catch us this time, they'll lock us both up."

His face grew dark. "A son obeys his father. If I tell you to work, Benno, you will work."

"I'll work, Papa, I will. When you play your concertina, I'll dance. The people will give money, you'll see. It'll be fine."

I waited for him to get angry, but he didn't. I waited for him to shout at me, or get to his feet and hit me, but he didn't. He sat in his chair, saying nothing. And that frightened me more than anything.

That night we had no supper. I didn't even have a candle so I could read my book. When it grew dark, we lay down on the mats, Papa in one corner and me in another. I felt like chalk dust on a blackboard.

At the front of Mistress Dreiwatter's classroom, there had been a blackboard. In the morning, it was washed clean, and when the children wrote their sums or their spelling words on it with a stick of chalk, the numbers and letters were sharp white against the black. Then, when they were done, the children erased their work. The numbers and letters disappeared, but the chalk dust stayed. At the end of the day, the blackboard was gray, and it was hard to see the numbers and letters. As I lay on my mat, I tried to think of what was coming, but all I could see was chalk dust.

The next morning, I dressed in only my shirt and trousers. I took my old cap, but I left my boots and stockings and jacket in our room. There was no need now for me to look like a proper boy.

"Today," Papa said, almost smiling, "there will be a parade—schoolchildren marching, musicians, acrobats. We will work there. The parade will be our look-away. The work will go well."

"No, Papa. I meant what I said. I won't do the work anymore. When we go to the parade, the people will give me their money. But I won't take it from them."

Papa's face darkened, but he did nothing. Before he went to prison, if I'd said no to him, Papa would have struck me. This wasn't the Papa who could make me feel icy-cold with fear, who could make me feel warm with happiness. This Papa made me feel sad.

In the city, crowds were gathering, waiting for the parade to start. Papa played his concertina and I danced. I smiled like the sun, spinning my arms and legs like a whirligig. I danced faster and faster, until I couldn't see anything around me, until I couldn't even think. People stopped and watched and some of them dropped coins into my cap. When we went home that night, we had enough coins to buy a loaf of bread, a chunk of cheese, and a stub of candle.

The next day, when we left the Stalls in the morning and were walking toward the city, I imagined that I was still a proper boy, clean all over, with my hair cut short, soft leather boots, and a blue jacket with shiny buttons. I walked on the sidewalk, my head up. Until I saw a lady or a gentleman. Then I remembered that I was just the same as I'd been before. Except for one thing—now I could read.

I read everything—street signs on buildings and shop signs in windows. I read the bills posted on walls. Each night, walking home, I picked up newspapers from the street. All that week and the next, the chalk dust spread itself over everything. But back in our room, reading the newspapers, the chalk dust was washed away.

One afternoon, we had stopped on a street corner only

a few blocks from the Central Market. For three days before, it had rained, the kind of light, chilly rain that comes in autumn, when people hurry along the street, not looking anywhere but straight ahead. But today the sun was shining and Papa was smiling. People were glad to stop for a moment, to listen to the gay concertina, to drop some coins into the cap of a skinny little kid whirling in time to the music.

I was still whirling when Papa suddenly stopped playing. He was looking toward the end of the street. A policeman in a blue uniform, the sun glinting off his brass buttons, was moving quickly toward us.

"Run, Benno!" Papa's voice was low and sharp. "Run!"

At Papa's order, my body quickened, ready to flee. But my brain had suddenly quickened also, and I realized we didn't need to run.

"He can't arrest us, Papa. We're only playing a concertina and dancing on a street corner. He can't arrest us for that. He'll only tell us to move on."

I took Papa's arm and began leading him away, as though we hadn't even seen the policeman and it didn't matter if we had.

"Benno!"

Officer Pikche's voice rang out from behind us, running through me like cool water. I spun around. Officer P. was not two paces from me, the corners of his mustache turned up in a wide grin.

Papa grabbed my shoulders. "Come with me, Benno!"

As Papa said that, Officer P.'s mustache drooped down and his mouth dropped open. I guess he realized that this must be my papa, but not anymore the papa who could knock me to the ground, the papa who needed two policemen to chain his hands behind his back.

I stepped in front of Papa. Officer P. shouldn't be looking at him like that. I wanted to take Papa away, to take him home. But I also wanted to stay where I was, to look at Officer P.'s face, hear him talk to me again.

"Benno, don't go, please." Officer P.'s voice was begging.

Behind me, Papa had his hands tight on my shoulders, but I could feel his body shaking.

"It's all right, Papa," I said. "Officer Pikche can't arrest you. You've done nothing wrong." I said that loud so Officer P. would be sure to hear me.

Officer P. wound his arms tightly around me and pulled me to his chest. The brass buttons of his uniform pressed into my cheek. Tears stung my eyes. It was because of the buttons.

"Let my son go! You can't arrest the boy for dancing on the street. Let go of him." Papa's hands were trying to pull me away, but Officer P. held me fast.

I squeezed my eyes shut. In my mind, I saw my bear's brown eyes looking at my face. I wished I could run back to her, rest my head against her rough fur, and feel nothing but the rocking of her breath.

Officer P. loosened his hold on me. As I wriggled free, Papa stepped beside me.

"Papa," I told him, "Officer Pikche has come to arrest me, not you. The schoolmistress says I stole her purse. But he can't arrest you."

I held out my hands to Officer P. so he could put the shackles on them. But Papa brushed my hands away.

"Haven't you made enough trouble for us, policeman?" Papa's voice was like a drum. "You sent me to prison. You took away our bear. You will not take my son."

Papa grabbed my wrist to lead me away, but I pulled back.

"I haven't come to take your son," Officer P. said. Then he turned toward me. "Benno, we know you didn't steal the purse."

"What purse?" Papa shouted. "Benno has stolen nothing today!"

"He means the teacher's purse, Papa." Now I was shouting, too. "Officer P., that's what you told me the day I ran away. You said you believed that I didn't steal Mistress's purse. But just the same, you and the other men came looking for me in the forest. You came to arrest me and bring my bear back to the zoo." My face was burning hot. "Well, go ahead. Arrest me now," I said. "At least you can't take my bear."

"Benno, look at me."

Officer P. had a way of talking that made me do what he said. I looked up at him.

Officer P. knotted his eyebrows. "I didn't come to the forest to arrest you," he said. "I came to tell you that the real thieves had been arrested. They've already been sent to the Public Residence for Wayward Youths."

"Who? Who's been arrested?"

"It was three boys—Bogwald and Erdweiss and Petrolin. They're the ones who took the purse."

"How did you find out? Mistress believed it was me."

"But I believed it wasn't. When we found your note, Kat and I were beside ourselves with worry. I went to the Stalls to see if you'd returned there, and while I was gone, your friend Niera came to the bakery, looking for you. She burst into a story about some creatures she called Toad and Grub and Snort and something about pencils and tops and coppers. Missus P. couldn't make any sense of what the child was saying."

"But I gave those things back. I—"

"I know you did—let me finish."

I looked at Papa. He was twisting his fingers through his beard.

"When I got back, the child had calmed enough that we could put together the bits and pieces of her story. Niera was convinced that three other boys had stolen the purse, knowing you would be blamed.

"I had her tell me the boys' real names and where they lived. I went first to Erdweiss's home, simply to ask him about the purse. But when he saw me in my uniform, he began sniveling and saying, 'I didn't take the purse, Toad did.' I was growing angrier by the moment. I marched Erdweiss to Bogwald's house, and Bogwald insisted that it had all been Petrolin's idea, that the other two had given Petrolin all the money. Petrolin never said a word. He didn't have to. I found him stuffing himself with sweets he'd bought with the stolen money. He hadn't even bothered to hide the purse."

"But if you weren't going to arrest me, why did you come looking for me in the forest?"

"I was coming to tell you that everything was all right. I wanted to take you back home."

As Officer P. said those words, Papa stamped his foot against the cobblestones. "No!" he shouted. "Benno is my blood, not yours. His home is with me. Come, Benno. Come with me now." Papa pointed in the direction of the Stalls.

"I have to go with my papa," I said. My voice came out very soft.

"Wait, Benno." Officer P. began tickling my hair with his fingers. He looked sideways at Papa. Then he took my face in his hand. "I'm sure your papa would want good things for you."

"My boy has everything he needs. He wants nothing from you." Papa's face was dark with anger.

"Officer P., I—" I wanted to say something more, but the words wouldn't come out. "I have to go."

I followed Papa out of the market.

THE NEXT NIGHT we were in our room, eating our supper, Papa sitting on the chair and me on the floor, when someone knocked on our door.

Papa shouted, "Leave us alone! There's nothing left for you to take."

Whoever it was kept knocking. I got up and opened the door. Missus P. was standing there, tall and straight.

"Benno," she said, and reached out to me.

I felt Papa's eyes on us, and I backed away from her quickly.

All sorts of thoughts were whirling in my head, like scraps of paper in a windstorm. I felt good, seeing Missus P. But I knew Papa would be angry that she had come, and I didn't want her to see our room. I didn't want her to see me dirty and barefoot. But I wanted to talk to her, tell her everything that had happened.

Then I heard Papa's chair scraping, his footsteps behind us.

"Did you come for your book?" I asked quickly. "I'll give it back to you."

"No, Benno, you keep the book. I want you to have it. May I come in?"

"No, not now. It wouldn't be good now."

"Please, Benno, I'd like to talk with you and your papa."

Papa? Why did she want to talk to Papa? Did she think Papa was making me steal again?

Papa was behind me, blocking the way into the room.

"Who is this? Who is this woman?"

"Papa, this is Missus Pikche. Officer Pikche's wife."

"Tell her to go away. I will not talk to her."

He walked to the window and turned his back to us.

I hurried to the corner where I slept, picked up the storybook, and put it into Missus P.'s hands.

"Please keep it, Benno. I want you to have it." She looked over at the broken chair. "May I sit down?"

"Here." I grabbed the chair and set it down next to her.

"Thank you, Benno."

Missus P. sat straight up in the chair, her hands folded in her lap. She began speaking to Papa's back.

"Sir," she said, "I have a bakery, a small one. I make breads, rolls, some cakes."

I felt ashamed and wished he would turn around.

"When Benno lived with us, he helped me. I still need a helper, someone to carry in the sacks of flour, lift the heavy crocks, do the scrubbing and sweeping. Benno was so good at the work that I was able to do more baking than before. Since he's gone, I really could use someone. Sir, I'd like to offer you the job."

She stopped speaking for a moment. When he didn't answer, she went on.

"We have a room in the attic. It was Benno's room. The room's clean and light, lots of fresh air. You and Benno can share it. You'd have all your meals with us. We can pay you a wage besides. When Benno lived with us, I was teaching him how to bake. I could teach you, too. And then, when my bakery grows, I'll be able to pay you more."

Papa still stood with his back to Missus P., saying nothing.

"Papa," I said, "if we went there, we wouldn't have to work on the streets."

Papa turned to me. "I will not work for this woman."

He should not have spoken like that in front of Missus P.

"Missus P.—"

Papa cut in. "Go home," he said to her. "Go home to your policeman. Leave. We don't need you or your money. Go."

Missus P. stood up and walked toward the door. Her eyes were begging me, like my bear's eyes when she didn't want me to leave the forest. The late-day sun slanted behind Missus P. through the doorway. I looked back at Papa, sunk deep in his own darkness.

Before Missus P. left and shut the door, I heard her say softly, "We love you, Benno."

22

Beginning

THE NEXT MORNING, black clouds blew across the sky. By noon, a sharp rain was falling. People on the street looked past us, their eyes on the store or the house they were hurrying to. We'd have few coins tonight, perhaps only enough for a loaf of bread. Papa was in a black mood. And so was I. I didn't want to dance in the street, go back at night to an empty room, lie stiff in the dark with knots of hunger in my belly and only a stub of candle to read by.

I had made a terrible mistake, and because of it, Papa had gone to prison for seven months. But in those months, everything had changed.

I stopped dancing, and Papa gave me a hard look.

"Papa, there's still time to go to the Pikches before dark. Please, Papa. Let's go now."

Papa put down his concertina and grabbed my arms in his big hands. I looked straight back at him. My eyes were even with his.

He let go of my arms, picked up his concertina, and shut me out. Once, I would have been begging Papa to let me back in, to take me back again. But not now. I didn't want to go back, to be shut inside with him.

"Papa?"

He didn't answer.

"I'm going, Papa."

Papa said nothing.

I started walking toward the Middle Bridge, listening for Papa's steps behind me. I'd never done this before. Two days ago, I hadn't gone with Officer Pikche. I'd stayed with Papa. Last night, I hadn't gone with Missus P. I'd stayed with Papa. Was he thinking I'd come back? Was he thinking about me at all?

The rain ended. At a kiosk a man picked up a newspaper and took out a coin to pay for it. The coins! I still had the coins from the day's work. I ran back, my heart drumming in my chest.

Papa was in the same place, his cap upside down on the ground, playing his concertina. He didn't look at me. Didn't he see me? Or had he shut himself inside his wall of ice? Papa played faster and faster, smiling and tapping his feet, but no one stopped.

Then, very slowly, as though the rain was washing the

chalk dust from my head, I began to see what I needed to do.

"Papa," I said, dropping the coins into his upturned hat, "I came back to give you the money."

"Dance, Benno," Papa muttered.

"No, Papa. I won't dance."

"Again you say no to me, to your papa?"

He went on playing his concertina. I stood and watched him. He played until the sun was low. Then he folded his concertina, picked up his hat, and started toward home. I walked beside him. He didn't speak to me, and he didn't look at me.

When we got to our room, Papa slumped into his chair, his eyes lowered. I stood in front of him.

"Papa, listen to me. I've thought of a way we won't be hungry anymore."

Now Papa's eyes flashed at me.

"We won't be hungry, you tell me?" he snarled. "While I was in prison, you freed the bear. When I came back, you would not do the work anymore. We don't need the bear, you said—you would dance. And today, first you walked away from me, and then you would not dance. Where will this money come from? Will it come from that book you read every night? Is there a picture in that book of money dropping from the sky?"

A fly buzzed through the open window. An ugly little thing, with skinny, twitching legs, and eyes everywhere.

The fly circled Papa's head. He reached out his huge hand to swat it, but he was too slow.

"They have filled your head with nonsense, those people. They have turned you into an imbecile."

Yes, they'd filled my head. But not with nonsense.

"Papa, that job Missus P. offered you in her bakery—"

"I'll never take her job. Never!" Papa spat the words at me.

"All right, Papa. You won't take the job. I will. I'll work in the bakery, just like I did before. But this time, Missus P. will have to pay me for the work. She said she would pay you—well, I'll ask her to pay me instead."

"I won't take money from a policeman and his wife."

A lick of anger flamed hot in me. "No, Papa. *You* won't take their money. *You* won't have to take anything from them. And I won't either. I'll work for the money. When I worked on the streets, I gave you the money I took from people. When you got out of prison, I gave you the money people gave me for dancing. From now on, I'll give you the money the Pikches pay me for helping in the bakery. You'll get money for playing your concertina, and between us, we'll have enough. More than we ever had. When winter comes, Papa, we'll be able to move out of this room, maybe even back to our old room."

"Yes," Papa was muttering. "Our old room was better. That is where we belong."

No, Papa, I thought. I don't belong there anymore. But

you do. Papa could never go to the Pikches. I could see that.

But from now on I'd be going to the Pikches every morning, helping Missus P. with the baking, taking Missus P.'s good lunch with me to school.

School! I could go to school again. Niera had told me that when we went on to the next grade, we'd have a new teacher. I hoped the new teacher would have a shelf of books.

"Tomorrow morning early, Papa, I'll go to the Pikches and tell them I'll work for them." I looked out the window, at the rain shining on the rooftops. "Papa, it rained today. Tomorrow, when I finish work, we could go to the woods and pick mushrooms."

Papa said nothing.

The fly landed on the windowsill, rested for a moment, then flew off into the air.

I could fly away, too. I could go up in a basket, hanging from a great balloon. I'd fly over the River Resier, over the River Murin, out over the forest. Perhaps my bear would look up and see me high above her in my balloon. She'd stand up tall, stretching her neck toward the sky, and the sun would turn her fur to gold.

I'd be about to call to her when she'd lower her paws to the ground and look down. Why? Had she already forgotten me? She'd nuzzle something beside her—a fat little cub. My bear would want me to see her cub, to know that she wasn't alone. Then she'd stand up tall again, and the little cub would stand up, too, its front paws resting on my bear's hind leg, and it would look up at me in the balloon.

"I'm Benno," I'd call down to the cub. "When your mama was as little as you, I took care of her. Then when she got big, we took care of each other."

My bear would still be looking up at me. I had to tell her something, too—something I had never told her before. "I love you, Bear." The words would come out soft, but I knew my bear would hear them.

And then I'd float on, my bear and her cub growing smaller and smaller, until I couldn't see them anymore.

It could all happen. My bear might have a cub. I could fly away in a balloon. But even if I never did, someday I was going to go far beyond the forest.